BLUE

Blue

D. Lee Cardwell

D&D

For my family:
Donna, Christian, and Luke

1

March 29, 1988

B-dum.

B-dum.

B-dum.

The damp morning air swallowed the faint gasps of the spent young man.

B-dum, B-dum, B-dum.

The tender grass of early spring glistened with the first hint of sunlight. A blurred yellow-green hue was the first thing the young man saw when he opened his eyes. Carolina pines dotted the landscape. Deer held a fixed gaze from the edge of the misty woods. Birds sang. The smell and taste of the salty marsh air still surprised him. His senses awoke, and the gloom of morning fog signaled the finality of the night's horror.

B-dum. B-dum. B-dum.

The rhythmic beat was heavy and it thumped like a bass drum in his ears. He was exhausted; his mind was not yet capable of processing the details of the previous night. Depleted, his naked body slumped against the base of the tree. His pale skin shined from the damp air like polished marble. He wiggled his limp arms behind the tree, but the tape was still tightly wrapped. He had more leverage on his feet, and the gray duct tape had loosened, but just a little. Without the use of his hands, he remained helpless.

It was early on a Sunday morning. In the distance, he saw the first arrival at New Hope Baptist Church. It was an elderly woman wearing a navy dress and a light pink sweater. She was trying to juggle what appeared to be her Bible, her purse, and a cane as she got out of her car and began inching her way toward the church.

"It can't be an old woman," he thought aloud, then almost laughed at the ridiculous mental image of the woman trying to make her way to him, using her cane to clear a path. He figured he would probably be dead of starvation by the time she finally got to him.

Once she was inside the church, he realized it was probably a mistake to have ignored her. He mustered the courage to shout out to the next arrival. He felt shame and embarrassment for sure, but weighed his options and quickly concluded that a choice had to be made.

"Help! Help! Please, help me!"

His nightmare was near an end. As the man approached, the boy recognized the face. He had hoped for little fanfare. He hoped for kindness and discretion from a stranger. Instead, Cole was rescued by Alan Jaymes.

2

July 3, 1970

Ann Banks stepped off a Greyhound bus onto a platform in San Diego, California. She was exhausted from the long trip. From her home in rural Ohio, she had narrowed her choices for relocation to Cape Canaveral in Florida or San Diego. The Apollo moon landings had recently captivated the nation, and when her widowed mother unexpectedly passed, Ann found herself nearly broke, alone, and without the opportunities of her male peers. She sold the family farm, but her youthful inexperience made her a target of the local real estate shark. She accepted a lowball offer, took the equity, and gave herself a firm deadline of three months.

Ann saw her only real talent in the mirror. Like girls of her era, she was expected to sew, cook, and clean just like her mother had done. Ann had not mastered these skills. Not even close. She had even struggled with the home economics curriculum at her county high school.

Boys had flirted with her from an early age, and she realized that she had a certain appeal that the other girls seemed to lack. Perhaps it was her auburn hair and green eyes that were perfectly proportioned around the bridge of a cute, yet distinct, nose. Her lips were fuller than average, and when they parted, she revealed a beautiful smile. Her wardrobe was limited, as Ann had to help her mom with groceries. She bought her own clothes with the Social Security benefit she received after her father died.

Ann knew it was time to look for a job, and she was committed to not settling for any "housewifing" position. She wanted a man who would provide her with security. He needed to be handsome, too. The prospects of a romantic entanglement with an astronaut were the most appealing, but she decided that her odds were better with a Naval officer. The afternoon after the farm sale closed, she cashed her check, bought a one-way bus ticket, and made her way to Southern California.

Her first night was spent in a hotel. The next day, she asked around, then hopped on a local bus, and made her way to the part of downtown where the sailors hung out. As the bus pulled away, she was almost immediately approached by a man in a white leisure suit.

"You new in town, sweetheart?" Ann didn't respond. "Do you need a job, sugar?" he asked.

Ann looked past him and saw an assortment of girls lining the street as she replied, "I am not that desperate."

"Too bad, baby! You would make a killing. Look at all these sailors giving you the eye," the pimp said.

Ann saw the sailors in their white uniforms. They didn't seem to be officers. She asked, "Are these officers?"

The greasy man answered, "Oh, I see. No, these are all enlisted dudes. You're looking for something in the higher-rank department, huh? Go three blocks east and check out a joint called *Harry's*. It will be full of girls like you later tonight. Most of my girls traveled down that road for a while, too. See what that got 'em? You know where to find me."

"Thanks for the help, but you won't see me again."

The pimp stared at Ann as she walked away and said to himself, "Mm, Mm. Probably not."

3

Mike Levy was not a member of the "Me Generation." He finished college in 1967 on a NROTC scholarship and joined the Navy as a commissioned officer. Lieutenant Levy spent a year split between San Antonio, Texas, and the Naval Weapons Station in Charleston, South Carolina, where he started his career in nuclear weaponry. He was stationed in Japan for two years before his current assignment to the San Diego Naval Base.

Mike was a little taller than the average Navy man, but he had the body type that would fit neatly into tight quarters on a submarine. He had received only exemplary marks from each physical test that the Navy required. He was naturally strong and coordinated. He was intelligent, but his greatest attribute was confidence. Mike could have been summa cum laude at Penn State, but his constant pursuit of the coeds held him back. Women had always kept him from maximizing his potential.

Mike decided that once in San Diego, he would finally search for a girl to "get to know." He saw many of his buddies fall prey to women that did little to hide their intent. His father had warned him, and, so far, Mike had steered clear of being wrangled into a relationship. Although he was nothing like the generation of the younger enlisted men, he did benefit from the sexual freedoms that women, at least those in California, were now eager to explore. Mike enjoyed his one-night stands and had never engaged in a relationship that lasted for more than a week. He loved all women, but he had a preference for redheads.

He spent most of '70 bar-hopping and picking up women, failing to deliver on the promise he made to himself. His favorite haunt was a bar on the corner of J Avenue and Fifth Street called *Harry's*. On the 4th of July in 1970, he watched the fireworks from a pier with some Navy buddies. Afterward, he and a few others ventured east a few blocks and found a surprisingly sparse *Harry's Bar*. The women outnumbered the men two to one, so Mike surmised that he would have his pick. As he sat at the bar and surveyed the offerings, a young, auburn-haired girl scrambled for the stool next to his, just beating out a blonde who looked like she should've been working for the hustler at the bus stop. Mike saw the ruckus for the stool and turned toward the girl now seated next to him, and chuckled.

"Looks like you won. Or maybe you lost. Only time will tell, I guess. I'm Mike. Haven't seen you here before," he said.

"No, I just moved here yesterday." Ann moved her eyes to make sure he had at least two full bars on his uniform. They were silver. This was her minimum requirement for rank. She could certainly check off the handsome requirement. He was a classically tall, dark, and handsome lieutenant. He reminded her a little of James Bond, but with a more narrow face and a shorter haircut. He would have been perfect if only he had been an astronaut.

"My name is Ann. Ann Banks. It is nice to meet you, Mike." Ann flashed her best smile and Mike's chest pounded.

"Mike Levy. You sure are beautiful, Ann."

"Levy? Where does your family come from?"

Mike was puzzled that she would pivot to that. Her green eyes had him captivated though, so he was happy to answer, "Ireland. But I was born in Connecticut. How about you?"

"Born and raised in Ohio. My mom's side was from Ireland, too. She passed away last month. I decided it was time for a change, so I thought I'd try California. Are you stationed here or just in port?" Ann was eager to carry the conversation along.

"I am stationed here. Been here for almost a year. I really like it. Irish, huh? That explains that lovely hair you have."

Ann blushed a little. She realized that with their shared Irish descent, they had at least one connection. She couldn't think of the next thing to say. Mike had far more experience, and her naivety excited him even more. He realized from the pinkening tone on her face that flattery was going to be the tool he would use to bed her. He continued, "And those green eyes just sparkle."

Ann tried to gather herself. "Thank you. You are a very handsome man, too. I bet you get all the girls."

"Right now, I only see one woman in here that interests me." He leaned in and whispered into her ear, "Let's get out of here."

Ann didn't want to appear too easy, but his swoon was too great. She would put up a mild fight, but they both knew they would sleep together that night.

Mike rolled out of bed the next morning and saw Ann draped with his bedspread. He thought to himself *'Oh my, this one is dangerous.'* Twenty minutes later, he stepped out of the bathroom and dressed in his uniform. Ann was awake and smiling at him. "Mike Levy, you are quite the lover. But somehow, I think you already know that."

"I haven't had any complaints. I have to be at the base in thirty minutes. You can make yourself some coffee if you like. I'll get some on the way. Stay for as long as you like. Just lock the door when you leave," Mike had rehearsed and performed the words as frequently as an actor in a Broadway play.

Mike's delivery and pitch were perfect, and Ann was not experienced enough to know what it all meant. She took 'stay for as long as you like' literally. When Mike returned at five-thirty, he was surprised to find her standing over a stove among the mess she had made. "You're *still* here," he said rhetorically.

"Yes, I wanted to make you supper. I went home and changed and picked up some groceries for a nice home-cooked meal. But, I have to warn you that I am not much of a cook." Ann eagerly replied.

Mike calculated a reply. "Looks good to me. What's for dessert? You, I hope."

Ann was blushing again. Mike choked down Ann's chicken casserole as they got to know each other. He learned more about Ann's family. She was an only child and her father preceded her mother in death. Mike was keenly aware of her vulnerability.

After dinner and conversation, Mike began to clear the table. Ann was perfectly content to leave the mess until later, but she could tell it was important to Mike. She mostly used the time to accidentally bump into him and brush his shoulders with her hands as she politely said, "Oh, excuse me." The last of the dishes were put away, and she turned and found Mike's gaze. "Are you ready for your dessert?"

Mike took her hand and led her back to his bed. He reached into the drawer of his bedside table and pulled the last condom from the drawer. "Last one. Lucky you."

Ann was lucky. She had been willing to pierce each and every condom in the place with the sewing needle she bought at Woolworth's that afternoon. She happily found only one left in the drawer where he had retrieved another the night before. She didn't want to compete with an outbreak of Levy babies, so she limited that risk and ignored the box in the medicine cabinet.

Mike rolled over at 7:30 the next morning and found Ann again draped in the bedspread. "I have to run some errands today. I have a two-week training cruise and I'm leaving tomorrow. Can I drive you home?"

Ann smiled at the prospects of Mike but realized she had not yet hooked him. She realized he was aroused by her naivety and said, "Well, I am staying at a hotel for now. I need to find a place. I have no clue what to do. Since you know the area so well, do you have time to help me?"

Mike tried to hide his feelings on the matter. He was reluctant and he felt his grip on freedom slipping. Somehow, he found her more beautiful now than when he first met her. To his surprise, he uttered, "Sure, but we have to go soon."

After a morning of searching, nothing seemed adequate or safe for her budget. After lunch, they searched further. Finally, Mike had an idea, and without thinking it through, he said, "I'll be gone for two weeks, home for a week, then gone for three months. You could stay here while I am gone. It's empty anyway. That will give you plenty of time to look around."

Ann didn't want to appear too eager. This was quickly escalating into fairytale land. She forced a reluctant pursing of her lips and said, "Are you sure?"

"Yes. Just keep it clean for me. Let's go get your bags from the hotel."

Ann found it difficult to hide her joy. Unexpectedly, Mike did, too.

4

After the training cruise, Mike returned to his apartment to find things a bit messier than he was accustomed to. He spent the week with Ann, and although he still found her attractive, his interest was waning. He realized they were from different backgrounds. He was a college-educated engineer, and she was a substandard housewife at best. Still, he enjoyed the bed they shared and that helped him navigate a week that seemed to drag on. By the last day, he was glad to be leaving for three months. When he returned, he would tell her she had to leave.

After Mike left for the second time, it was three weeks before Ann would bask in the glory of her success. Her breasts were sore, and she was late. After a quick trip to the local clinic, she had her confirmation; she was pregnant.

Mike returned hoping to find that Ann had vacated his apartment. The doctor had told her that she was nearly sixteen weeks along now. Her trim body did nothing to help mask the baby bump. She had rehearsed how she would deliver the news to Mike. She had to navigate the condom issue, and she was hoping he would accept the explanation. She prayed he would do the honorable thing.

Ann heard the door unlock. She stood tall as Mike entered the room. His eyes didn't seem to hide his disappointment in her presence. He forced a smile and said, "You didn't find a place yet?" As Ann turned, Mike saw her profile for the first time. After a lengthy pause, he asked, "Are you pregnant?"

This was not the way she rehearsed it. She instantly felt on the defensive. "Yes. I planned a better way of telling you, though. I don't know what happened. You always used protection, but the doctor said those are not always one hundred percent effective."

"This is *mine?*" Mike was shaken.

Ann shed a tear for dramatic effect and delivered a line that set the hook. "What kind of girl do you think I am? You are the only man I have ever been with."

Mike pivoted. He was going to be a father. He was surprised at how quickly he accepted it. The weeks passed and his feelings toward Ann grew. She was carrying his baby, yet he was still unfulfilled and realized his feelings were not love, but duty. For the baby's sake, he would suppress them.

5

January 1988

The snow was ankle-deep, but the driveway was already half-cleared. Cole worked quickly. He loved the purity of the first white snow, but after it was piled up, it changed to a dirty, gray eyesore. It was a cycle that repeated itself every winter.

"Put your cap and coat on *now!*"

Cole's copper hair had turned a deep brown from the sweat and the wet snow falling from the branches that hung over the drive. He raised his head and met his mother's eyes.

"I'm hot." His pale, freckled face glowed with heat and seemed polished by his sweat.

"At least cover your ears. They're red," Ann Levy said with more compassion.

"Yes ma'am." Cole reluctantly replied.

He knew that disrespecting his mother would mean having to listen to his father's stern corrections when he came home from the base. He put the cap on and pulled it over his ears. The driveway was soon clear and readied for the moving van that was scheduled for the next day. Everyone in the family looked forward to the move east to a milder winter and the larger city near the base. Everyone except Cole's older sister, Emily.

Emily was slightly taller than her mom, but still had her mother's markings. She had fair skin and red hair but it was less textured than her mother's hair. And like her father and brother, she had a naturally athletic build. She was lucky to inherit the soft features from her mom instead of the angular face of her father.

Crane is in the middle of Southern Indiana. It seems an obscure place to put a U.S. Navy base. Crane's existence relies on the U.S. Navy Support Center and the Naval Weapons Station. All the usual entrapments existed to keep everyone happy. There is Eagle View Golf Course, a bowling alley, youth sports, and various other activities. The only thing Cole would miss was Lake Greenwood.

In the summer, Cole and Emily would sometimes meet their father after work at the marina. The family owned a pontoon boat, and Cole liked fishing off the boat. Emily enjoyed lounging in the sun. The family had exactly one of those classic tri-fold loungers with a vinyl cord wrapped a billion times around an aluminum frame. Every time Emily rolled over, it looked like she had been flogged with wet noodles.

She and Cole managed a slight golden tan by the end of each summer. Their dad would insist on sunscreen on the few days a month he could meet them. Their fair skin would never really darken. Cole was more prone to a burn, and his freckles were more pronounced in the summer. He hated them. His hair turned strawberry blonde in the summer, just like their mom's. Emily was jealous because her hair never really changed with the sun. One Memorial Day, when she was younger, she poured half a bottle of bleach on it. She looked like a pumpkin and the family missed the town's big summer kickoff, a favorite of Cole's. He would eventually forgive her.

Mike Levy was harder on Emily than Cole. He had reason to be. He long suspected she found trouble–and he couldn't look past her strong resemblance to his wife. Cole knew that Emily had lost her virginity to the lifeguard at the marina last summer, a lanky boy with a big head and hair over his ears. Mike would have never approved of the hair.

Mike Levy was still a square jaw military man, true and true. After twenty-two years of service, his only change seemed to be in the color of his now-graying hair. Women were naturally drawn to him, but he hadn't swayed from his marriage since the family moved to Indiana. He was stern with his children, and resentful to still be stuck in a loveless marriage.

"Can I skip this haircut? I just want it *on* my ear," Cole would ask as part of a monthly routine just before the trip to the base barber shop.

"Nope. Stop asking and get in the car."

Mike did little to help Ann with the kids, but he always maintained complete financial control over the family. He rarely gave Ann enough money to effectively run the household. She siphoned off some from the little she was given and used it to drown her sorrows. They were not a poor family. Mike secretly socked away money like a squirrel gathering nuts for the winter—at least he thought it was a secret. Ann knew how much he made, and how little she had available in comparison. Money was one of many themes eating away at their marriage. Mike managed to keep the money hidden from the rest of the family as best he could. It was his divorce money.

Ann rarely left the home in Crane. She had only one true friend, and it lived in a bottle. She wanted to leave the day-to-day parenting to Mike. She went through the motions of trying to be a Navy wife and mom. She was only truly present when Mike couldn't be, but since their second tour in San Diego, Mike had not had an extended deployment to sea in nearly six years. She knew that would change once they hit Charleston. She had already begun to question her ability to manage without him.

The last boxes were packed. The driveway stayed cleared. It was a Saturday in January, so Cole and his father settled into their spots in the small family room. The Colts were playing the Browns in the first playoff appearance for the franchise since moving from Baltimore to Indianapolis. Frank Minnifield intercepted the Colts' quarterback, Jack Trudeau, and returned it 48 yards for a TD to seal the victory for Cleveland. Final score was 38-21. Soon after the game, the doorbell rang. Ann sat quietly in the kitchen sipping on a plastic glass full of her special tea as Mike opened the door.

"I'm here for the boat."

Mike Levy sold the pontoon boat for $700. He threw in Emily's tired old chair for free. Promises were made to buy a runabout when they got to Charleston. Emily knew it would never happen.

Ann spoke under her breath, "We'll never see that money again. Into the black hole, it goes."

Cole and Emily nodded in unison.

6

Mayflower Movers packed up the truck on Sunday. Mike had to report on Monday morning so the family situated themselves in the Chrysler minivan and got on the road about ten hundred. Ann made a room reservation for that night at the Foster Creek Inn, in Foster Creek, South Carolina. She would meet the movers Monday afternoon after getting a housing assignment from the Office of Navy Housing in the morning. The new digs were always clean, but she always insisted they needed further sterilization. "You don't know what kind of germs people may have left behind." Ann's ability to maintain the initial cleanliness she insisted on in each new home was always short-lived. She never left anything the way she found it. Her messiness and clutter were two of many triggers for Mike.

The planned route was to drive to Nashville and take I-40 east through the Smoky Mountains into North Carolina. A manageable trip of twelve hours. Especially when compared to the roughly twenty hours it took the family to drive from San Diego to Crane nearly five years ago. Cole and Emily picked at each other every mile of that trip.

Out of nowhere, Emily would scream, "Stop staring at me, idiot!"

Mike Levy would scream and threaten to stop the van. It was a threat that everyone knew could not be ignored. Cole would smile at her in the backseat. He had a gap in his front teeth as wide as a keyhole. Emily was twelve at the time. Cole was ten.

It seemed that every time the family moved, Emily was in the worst possible grade for a transfer. The move from San Diego was at the start of her 7th-grade year, halfway through middle school in Crane. Cole had finished grammar school in California and would have entered a new school anyway. In Crane, he would begin 5th grade in middle school. Charleston was an even worse transition for Emily. Her senior year would be at Foster Creek High School, home of 'The Gators.' The family had inquired about going to the newer school, Stanford High, home of 'The Knights,' but Berkeley County did not have open zoning. Mike Levy would not pay extra to rent a home in that school zone, despite a pay increase for his promotion to CWO5. Military housing was just fine for his family. They always seemed to live below his rank.

Ann learned not to argue with her husband. To Cole, the gator mascot must mean a nearby lake. He was unsure if the lake had any gators, but as long as they left his fish alone, he didn't care.

Cole had heard that Foster Creek had a good football program on par with the program of the crosstown rivals. He was now a sophomore and the snow-shoveling and other chores had made him lean and strong. He was not a fast runner, nor was he slow. As a rising junior, he would try out for receiver.

Cole worked out all summer to get ready for football tryouts at Loogootee High. In late July, the word came down from the base commander that the Levys would transfer from the Naval Weapons Station in Crane to the Charleston Naval Weapons Station. The orders were for an early September move. Chief Warrant Officer Levy called the AD at Foster Creek High and arranged for a later tryout for Cole. The schools were very accustomed to these requests and were almost always accommodating. Football was to the south what basketball was to Indiana and Kentucky. Even Foster Creek was not immune to the bug. The Gators had a no-cut policy for football, and Cole was excited about the move.

Emily was thrilled when a delay meant she could at least start her senior year at Loogootee. Cole was less thrilled because he had delayed his football career thinking he was going to move in the fall. By Thanksgiving, plans were "finalized" and the family would move and start the spring semester in Charleston. A week after the semester started, the family was on I-40 east of Nashville.

7

Commander Andrew McCaster assumed command of the Charleston Naval Weapons Station in the summer of 1985. His family lived in a large Georgian home on the base. Original brownstone brick had been painted a glossy white, and both of the porches and the shutters were painted a local color called Charleston Green. The color is black to almost anyone north of Broad Street in Charleston. In the front yard was a massive live oak with its lower branches diving downward toward the ground before arching upward. The longest branch was nearly as long as the tree was tall. The Spanish moss was confined to the upper reaches of the tree and the perimeter of the limbs. The fast-growing Carolina pines were abundant on the base, but the Commander's wife only wanted the oaks. The last of the pines in the yard was cut down in the fall of 1985 to make room for a backyard rose garden designed for hosting various parties.

The front yard could have been on the cover of *Southern Living*. In addition to the iconic oak, the yard had meticulously manicured azaleas, daylilies, and formal beds ironically mulched with pine straw. In early spring, the mixture of white, pink, and purple flowers flanked a narrow creek on the starboard side of the home. Too numerous to count, the established shrubs at the manor had a six-foot diameter with nearly the same height. The contrast of the evergreen plants against the painted white brick of the home made for a photo op any time of the year. Zoysia was the lawn of choice. It is a lush, emerald green creeping grass, and a heat-tolerant slow grower. The base golf course plugged its fairways with the stuff a few years ago and eventually, it took over the fescue. The base commander at the time insisted his lawn get the same plugs. He was not a horticulturist which was obvious when in his last spring as commander, he had the lawn mowed to the depth of the putting greens. He was then informed that the greens were bentgrass, not zoysia. Before he could change it, orders came in and the McCasters were running the show. The lawn was never threatened again, even by the rare frost from the mild coastal winters.

As spring rolls into summer, the blooms of the azaleas yield to another of the area's perennials, gnats. Or, as locals call them, "no-see-ums." In full bloom, the stealthy, flying teeth are worse than the mosquito. They are relentless. The critter's sting hurt just enough and was frequent enough to drive everyone inside.

Cookie McCaster lasted exactly one spring before the commander commissioned a screened porch. The porch had the customary shiplap flooring painted Charleston Green. The glossy, crimson rocking chairs reflected the black shiny floor paint. The McCaster children, Billy, and his older sister, Emma, got as much enjoyment out of the porch as did their mother. Billy was a handful. He wasn't an ADHD kid, but his energy and his self-entitlement prevented him from considering any point of view other than his own. Billy used his father's rank to his every advantage. This was going on long before he arrived at the Weapons Station.

Billy found his sweet spot in Charleston. The middle school he first attended was void of sports. Manningfield Middle had a large field behind it that served as Billy's kingdom before school and during recess prior to lunch. Billy was an instant hit with his classmates. Most of the students walked to the school from the nearby naval housing complex. The Weapons Station housed the kids of the higher-ranking commissioned officers, and these kids "rode the cheese" for the 3-mile trip. The school was part of the county school district but was located on U.S. Navy property. The student body was 100% military kids, and Billy was the chief brat.

Billy warmed up to his eighth-grade social studies teacher. Mr. Jaymes was young and only in his second year at Manningfield. He taught Billy social studies, and Billy taught him how to be one of the popular kids. Mr. Jaymes would play basketball with the 8th graders at recess. Finally, he felt like an elite athlete because could dominate 13- and 14-year-olds. He was so proud of himself when he was always on Billy's team. Alan Jaymes was now one of the jocks. He told stories to the kids of his glory days as a three-sport star athlete in Florence, South Carolina. He quarterbacked the football team, played the 3 spot in basketball, and occupied center field and the leadoff spot on the baseball team. Part of his new persona. The truth of these facts was that Mr. Jaymes had a basketball goal on a pole in his backyard and that was the extent of any sport he played in high school. Once, he tried out for the school musical, but after receiving a part, he chickened out and quit. He was an average high school student and a less-than-average college student. What he did have was an uncle who was the superintendent of schools in Berkeley County.

Billy was athletic and did not lack confidence in any respect. He was nearly always the center of attention. He wore clothes that were bought from department stores in nearby Northwoods Mall. Most kids got their clothes from the Navy Exchange or older siblings. Billy had light brown shaggy hair, brown eyes, a narrow nose, and a square jaw. Most middle school boys wanted to be his best friend. He played trumpet in the band, which meant he was always grouped in classes with the smart kids. The girls constantly flirted with him, but he was a late bloomer in that area and had little interest in more than himself.

Foster Creek High School was not 100% military. The following August, for the first time, Billy attended school with civilian kids. The kids living in Foster Creek were from a class that Billy had not seen before. They were largely poor, and they frowned on military kids, especially the privileged ones. The Navy paid for all but 15% of off-base housing. Most higher-ranking officers took advantage of the upgrade in the adjacent communities so their kids could attend the rival school in Ladson on the other side of Crowfield Plantation.

Billy played football and basketball every year of high school. By his junior year, partly because of attrition and partly because of an injury, Billy assumed the role of starting quarterback. The team made its usual playoff run before losing to powerhouse Summerville High in the state semifinals. Billy had an above-average arm but was not patient enough to wait for his receivers to run themselves open. Billy preferred to leave the pocket and scramble forward for a few yards. The Gators had a massive offensive line and, as such, had a great running game.

After the season, it was on to basketball. The team had never had the success of the football team, possibly due to the lack of a viable youth basketball program. After another dismal basketball season, Billy went back to off-season football workouts to get ready for spring practice and next season. It was early February before he noticed a new face in the room.

"Hey, Red!"

8

Billy turned to the kid beside him. "What's that kid's name?"
"Cole, I think."
"Thanks, Scrub!" Billy had trouble recalling the starting offensive lineman's name. In fact, he never even bothered learning it in the first place. 'Scrub' was his go-to for most of his classmates, teammates, and an occasional opponent.

"Hey, Red! Cole!" Billy barked across the room.

Cole was bent over the stool at his locker pulling up his Navy Exchange tube socks. When he realized Billy was talking to him, he angled his head left and looked over at Billy. Cole was not used to being called 'Red.' Everyone knew him as Cole back in Crane. Since moving to Foster Creek a couple of months ago, his afternoon outside workouts had begun to turn his hair into shades lighter than the darker copper color of winter hair in Indiana. Cole was shy, timid, and not yet comfortable in his new surroundings. He had yet to make a good friend, but he, like everyone, knew of Billy.

"What?" he said, exercising his thin lips to form a forced smile.

"Oh, my God! Coach! Coach! We don't have to share the endzone with the kickers anymore at practice." The coaches knew Billy well enough that they didn't have to ask why. The punchline would always come soon and usually at someone's expense. "We could put Cole here on the sideline and the kickers could practice kicking through that gap in his front teeth."

Cole took the temperature of the room and realized that most gave Billy at least a courtesy laugh. The coach simply said, "That's enough,

Billy." At this point, Cole decided to play along in hopes that this would soon stop.

"Funny!" Cole's response was disingenuous and delivered with little confidence. Cole was not ready to admit it was much worse before he lost his baby teeth. He couldn't even remember the last time someone mentioned it or looked at it funny.

Billy pounced, "Scrub, is that a frog in your throat?"

Cole's voice was like that of a seventy-year-old chain smoker. He had always had the gravel. At times, when he was embarrassed, his shy nature made it a little shaky, as well. Instead of responding this time, Cole's eyes shifted back to his socks. Billy took notice that he got under the new guy's skin.

"Oh, Red, this is going to be a fun spring." As Billy turned toward Scrub number three, he murmured, " I love messing with the new kids. It's just so easy. You remember when I took your virginity, right scrub?" Scrub number three half-smiled, but the other scrubs ignored it.

An assistant coach popped in the door and yelled, "On the track in five!" Cole ran out the door with shoes in hand. Billy loitered for a couple more minutes trying to milk the room for the last drops of what he viewed as a glorious achievement. With seconds to spare, Billy joined the group as the coach said, "Five laps, warm up!" There was no way Billy should have misread the stare of disapproval as he once again loitered before going to the field. The coach was already tiring. *Just be a leader.*

"Coach, why don't we stretch before we start running?" It came across as a smart-ass question, but Billy truly wondered why.

The coach replied, "Ever see a dog stretch before it runs after a squirrel?" For once, Billy had no response.

It did not take long for pods of runners to form, not because of pure differences in speed, but more out of friendships that developed in the spring. The track around the field was not in good condition, but it was still preferred over the conditions of the turf on the field. The summer months would be more competitive as the boys began jockeying for starting spots. Cole found himself in a larger pack of runners each and every day.

The packs stuck together for the body weight exercises. Billy never connected as to why he was rarely in a group of more than three boys. From his vantage point, all the scrubs were intimidated. Billy had been given a double portion of arrogance and confidence. Cole had been given a half-portion of confidence at best.

The Foster Creek football stadium and track were in the middle of a swamp. The city was given the land and after the sand had been dredged up to form a *solid* base, the school, and athletic fields were built. Just off campus was a brackish tidal creek called Foster Creek that feeds the Cooper River, which drains directly into the historic Charleston Harbor. There were coastal rains nearly every day in the spring and late afternoon thunderstorms even more frequent in the humid summer. The creek ran adjacent to the school and the road from the school to the Weapons Station. It was prone to flooding but would quickly recede after heavy rains. Cole experienced the swamp in the early spring. Cole would not experience the flying teeth in April.

9

On February 1, 1988, CPO Mike Levy boarded a nuclear submarine for a six-month tour to places he could never discuss. That was standard Navy policy. For the five years the family was in Crane, Mike had advanced training on nuclear weapons and all technical systems supporting them. He had not had a prolonged cruise since San Diego. Mike's days in Crane were spent maintaining technical equipment and systems. He also spent a lot of time in Navy classes trying to keep up with the new class of weapons and boats being built. It was more of a 7:00 AM - 4:00 PM job. Mike enjoyed the structure of the Navy and the controlled time he could spend with Cole and Emily.

Ann rarely joined any family outings, even when they lived in California. She had much more responsibility in San Diego when Mike was out to sea. Cole was in preschool then, so Ann planned a couple of outings a week with him after she dropped Emily off at school. Emily had always been part of the outings in the past and begged to go with them instead of tending to her 2nd-grade curriculum. One of Cole's only memories of those days was a trip to Palm Desert to a zoo. San Diego had a traditional zoo that the family loved, but Ann wanted Cole to see the animals more native to the desert. Cole remembered lots of snakes and little else. He did, however, remember seeing a roadrunner. He remembered how small the animal was in comparison to its cartoon representation. And the zoo didn't have a coyote.

The getaways were soon not enough to keep Ann challenged or happy. As with many Navy wives, to pass the time she developed a long-lasting friendship with a bottle of Mr. Jack Daniels. As soon as

Cole was old enough to recognize the scent of whiskey on her breath, he told his father and there were no more trips. Once both kids were in school, Ann and Jack would start their morning conversation at about 9:00 AM. Around 3:00 PM, the kids would arrive home from school. They were capable of making themselves a bologna sandwich. Ann was up from a nap by four in time to whip up dinner, served promptly at eighteen hundred. There was little conversation during dinner. The kids washed the dishes, then Mike took the kids to the park while Ann did a quick clean of the house, anxious to meet the odorless Mr. Smirnoff.

She vowed when they moved to Crane that things would be different, and for a while, they were. Mike had infrequent travel, and Ann found the smaller community more acceptable to her limited social skills.

After Mike Levy bought the pontoon, Ann found herself more alone in the afternoons as the kids would slip away to the nearby lake long before their father would get home. This allowed Ann to settle back into her daily dance with vodka. Once more, she told herself things would be different in Charleston. Ann snuck a drink on Saturday while Emily was in her room still crying over saying her last goodbye to her boyfriend, Rob, and Cole finished shoveling the driveway.

10

Only a few days passed before Emily and Cole quickly found something to do after school to stay out of their mom's way. Cole joined the football team and stayed until at least 1700 every day. Emily got a job at the Baskin-Robbins across the street from the high school. The Levys only had the minivan, and Mike Levy took it to work every day. The family lived on the northwestern side of the enormous housing complex, far away from the middle school but close enough to the high school where they would be able to walk. As high schoolers, the kids were expected to get themselves up, eat cereal, dress, and be at school on time. Mike left at 0630 and he woke them just before he left. Ann would usually sleep off her late-night date with Mr. Whatever's On Sale.

Ann was a liquor store whore willing to date any bottle with a reduced price tag. She was not alone. Many wives in Charleston learned to love the bottle. South Carolina had mini-bottles that could easily be hidden in a purse. Ann had heard that South Carolina was in the Bible Belt. It was a fact that Carolinians loved their spirits. Her neighbor, Janet, recently attended a WMU meeting in the Baptist Church and the Woman's Missionary Union quickly wrapped up their discussion of the success of the Lottie Moon Christmas Offering and adjourned to *Smuggler's Inn* in time for happy hour and three-for-one strawberry daiquiris.

Ann soon found the names on her bottles were not her only friends. The lonely women on Sunset Street would meet regularly, play cards, and DRINK. It wasn't long before Ann migrated toward them. Janet suggested the girls go away for a weekend in March.

"We have been here for two years, and I still have not been to downtown Charleston. My sister visited last summer and stayed downtown at *The Lodge Alley Inn*. She said it was near the Battery, Rainbow Row, The Old Market, and lots of bars and clubs."

"You had me at 'bars.' How much are we talking about here?" Ann added.

"If we all stay in one room, maybe $20 each? Plus spending money."

Ann seldom contributed to the conversations, but she was quick to the draw this time. "Count me in!" She was out of her chair and at the wall calendar. "How about the last weekend in March?"

"Works for me." The other ladies agreed with Janet.

All the husbands were out to sea so there would be no conflicts. No contact allowed, no permission, no problem. Thanks, Navy policy. All the women decided that their kids could either fend for themselves or have a sleepover somewhere else. Anywhere else.

Janet called, and the Lodge Alley Inn entered a reservation in the book for Levy, four guests, two doubles, smoking.

11

It took the principal at Manningfield Middle three years to downsize Mr. Jaymes out of his 8th-grade position. His uncle only agreed that the move to Foster Creek could be made because Mr. Jaymes now had tenure. Foster Creek had an opening for a world history teacher, and it was rare they would accept a candidate in the social studies department that could not coach a sport. Alan called his uncle again to thank him. The conversation ended so no doubt could be made as to the present state of his uncle's patience.

"I can't help you again, so don't screw this up!"

Mr. Jaymes was downright giddy to see that Billy McCaster was on his 3rd-period roll. The tail once again wagged the dog, and even though Mr. Jaymes had express authority, it wasn't long before Billy controlled third period. Billy elevated his status further when it was announced that he had *earnet-ish* the starting quarterback spot.

"Just like me," Mr. Jaymes announced to the class. He was still living the dream. Had he lasted for more than a year, he would have been ashamed when he learned that the first thing the principal asked his uncle was if he was able to coach football. His uncle relayed that Alan Jaymes had never played anything, and he should be limited to ticket sales and club sponsorships. The information was passed on to the coaches and a suitable pre-algebra teacher was hired to coach defensive backs.

On a random Tuesday morning in August, Billy sprung his trap. "Mr. Jaymes, did you watch the Panthers game last night?"

"I VCR'd it, so don't tell me anything about it. I am going to watch it tonight."

"OK, but I will just say that Green had a great game for the Packers."

"Cool. I love him. I have to review for Friday's quiz, so I can't really talk anymore about football right now."

It was all Billy could do not to laugh out loud with his classmates. The Monday night game was not between the Panthers and the Packers. Moreover, the Packers didn't have any player named Green on the roster. The next day, Billy ascended to alpha status.

"So did you see the game?"

"Amazing. Like you said, Green was spectacular! Billy, what are you doing?"

Billy had removed a bottle of Old Spice from his satchel and began to shake it around the desk. "It's a little smelly in here, Mr. Jaymes."

After a quick look around the room and confirmation from a few of Billy's scrubs, Mr. Jaymes seized the bottle and managed to empty most of the contents.

"Whew, I think we may have overdone that Billy. This is starting to give me a headache," Mr. Jaymes replied, still glowing over what he had done.

"*We may have over done it. Dude I got you to do that. Too easy.*"

"I am getting one, too," Tonya said, sensing a free period was on the horizon. Mr. Jaymes was at the door and spent five minutes fanning the door trying to remove the odor.

Mrs. Odom had 3rd-period planning and as she passed his room she said, "What are you doing and what is that smell?"

Five minutes later, a laughing Mr. Jaymes finished his story and turned toward the loud classroom. "Be quiet for a second. Hey now, you got to settle down. Is it better now?"

"No," said a collection of voices savoring their triumph.

Mr. Jaymes looked at Billy and laughed out loud. "OK, just a little more then." A few minutes later the door was closed and Mr. Jaymes positioned himself in the front of the room. "Well, that was an adventure." Most of the class was still otherwise engaged.

"Do you like Old Spice, Mr. Jaymes?" Billy was not yet ready to let it go,

"Well, I do, but I would never put that much on." Just as the class would start to settle down, Mr Jaymes would smile, look at Billy and say "Billy, I can't believe we did that." He was not yet ready to surrender his *moment*. Eventually, he began class, and 5 minutes later the bell rang. Mission accomplished.

Mr. Jaymes was like a caged mouse on a wheel. Billy held court at least 2 days out of each week. As the year passed, he recruited others to help with the distractions. It was clear to everyone, however, that Billy had to be vested for any plan to work, and no other class period could match the success of 3rd period.

On Sunday, the school gym became New Hope Baptist Church. As always, Alan Jaymes overstated the importance of his new job. The church paid a school employee $100 every Sunday to open the building and a few classrooms for Sunday School by 7:00 AM, turn on the AC or more rarely, the heat, and pull out the racks of stored metal folding chairs stored under the stage at the end of the gym. Church deacons would arrive soon after and begin transforming the gym into a worship center. Alan was always punctual but rarely arrived first. After the service, he helped put the chairs back on the rack to expedite his departure. For the rest of the approximate five hours, he would work in his room grading papers. He occasionally forgot to lock a classroom door or check that the toilets were flushed, the consequence of which was a simple reminder from a teacher or the custodian.

He quickly found out that the seasoned junior and sophomore teachers did not put Billy McCaster on the same pedestal as he did. Still, he would matter-of-factly recall the very funny thing Billy said in class. He was immune to the eye-rolling of his peers and apparently never heard the whispers of the English teacher at the other end of the table, "I don't let him get away with that nonsense in my class."

Mr. Jaymes was certain his daily banter with Billy was the highlight of his students' day. Truth be told, when the bell rang, Billy didn't give a rat's ass about anything that happened in 3rd period. This was high school and Billy had already at least marginally matured. He only engaged with Mr. Jaymes cause he knew he could and he hated history.

In January, there was significant turnover in the student body. Most transfers were made in the summer, but running a close second was the winter break. Mr. Jaymes was eager to see how his rosters changed when the new semester started. To his surprise, he lost only a half-dozen kids to withdrawals, and three transferred to a different teacher. Alan's spin was all positive.

"I even have smaller classes and not a single new student. Jackpot!," he declared boisterously in the teacher's lounge during lunch.

As was often the case, he failed to capture the true message that kids wanted out of his class and the guidance office would not saddle new students with his class. The other world history teacher was soon at the state capacity of thirty-five in each class. Any new transfers into FCHS would have to suffer through Mr. Jaymes' dog and pony show.

12

Schedule:	Levy, Cole	10	Spring 1988
1sr	English	A14	Mrs. Rollins
2nd	World History	B12	Mr, Jaymes
3rd	Biology	B6	Mrs. Nichols
4th	Study Hall	Audi	Staff
5rh	Lunch A		
	Homeroom B	B12	Mr. Jaymes
6th	Geometry	B18	Mrs. Phillips
7th	Mechanical Drawing	I2	Coach McDonald

Dismissal:
Bus Riders: 1:58 PM
Walkers:2:03 PM
Drivers:2:10 PM

Cole had hit the daily double, and that was not a good thing. He drew Mr. Jaymes not once, but twice. He did not exactly know what Mechanical Drawing was, but he was told by his guidance counselor that it was the only shop class that had space.

"It's like architecture," Mrs. Darden explained. As usual, the guidance counselor was clueless. Cole spent nearly a month learning to draw letters in-between two tiny horizontal lines. Coach McDonald called it single-stroke lettering and insisted it was a thing. In February, he drew 3-dimensional figures to scale using T-squares and a triangle. Two-point perspectives soon followed and Cole was hooked. It was his favorite class and Coach McDonald was his favorite teacher. Being the last period of the day, Coach allowed the boys to leave a little early to dress for workouts.

Before that first encounter with Billy in the locker room, Cole had heard more than he cared about. Mr. Jaymes had portrayed Billy as the coolest, most athletic, together junior since...well, himself back in his glory days. Some days, Mr. Jaymes actually did teach a little history. It was dull, but at least the time passed more quickly. Mr. Jaymes' stories were meant to be impromptu but Cole and his classmates always felt they were a little rehearsed. Cole felt that he learned more from his teacher in a week at Loogootee than he had in two-and-a-half months from Mr. Jaymes.

After some of the basketball team joined the football team in early March, the coaches began to plan for spring practice. A couple of weeks later, they had the customary days in shorts and shells, and finally eighteen days of full pads. Cole would be given his shot at receiver, as was his preference. Coach McDonald was skeptical based on his height, frame, and sadly his skin color. His timed sprints were just good enough to get a look.

"OK, time to see what we got." Some of the starting receivers were running track or playing baseball, so Cole was the "starter" at the slot to run the complete offense. Coach Selby called the first play. Cole stood in the huddle, left arm draped around his waist, right arm hanging limp to the side, head angled toward his drooped right shoulder. Coach McDonald assessed the body language and took a mental note that Cole likely had no clue what to do, and the play would be to him. The team clapped and broke the huddle. Cole lined up in the slot on the right but on the line of scrimmage. The tight end signaled him back two yards. Cole did not exactly know why, but he followed the instructions. He moved on to the sight of the ball movement. Forward three steps, he turned his hips left. The defender crossed his feet and turned to follow. Cole planted his left foot, shot his left arm across his body, and cut back to the right. It was then that Billy hit him in the hands with the ball. Cole then arced slightly left to avoid a reaching linebacker. Instinctively, he slapped thirty-two's hands down and moved forward. The other backer closed in from the left. Fifty-six's original assignment was to cover the crossing tight end. He had recovered and closed in on Cole. Cole moved the ball from his left to high-and-tight on the right. He extended his left arm and gave the backer a jolt on the shoulder. Shoveling Indiana snow from the driveway had added some unexpected strength to the lean muscles. A few more steps, and he was blindsided by a safety.

At first, he considered just laying in the spongy soft grass for a while. He was not expecting the tackle to hurt. He decided to bounce up and, to his surprise, the play went for thirteen yards. The defensive coaches all started yelling at the defense about assignments and excuses. Coach McDonald simply ran up to Cole, slapped the top of his helmet, and simply said "Cole, you're going to be alright."

"Good throw, Billy!" Coach Selby barked with a gruff voice from the sideline.

The staff planned for lots of throws to backs, slot receivers, and tight ends next season. Everyone remembered the limitations of Billy's pocket patience.

Back in the huddle, Cole's body language was better. No longer slouching with hands on hips, he leaned into the huddle expecting to hear Billy call the next play. "I made that easy for you, Red! You didn't have to do much except put your hands out. Perfect pass." Billy called the next play. It was to be a screen pass. As the offensive lineman let the pass rushers through, Billy was to dump the pass off to a back that circled around to their flank. It was a dance. The offensive lineman would shift over in front of the back and escort him downfield, mowing down any defenders left in their path. The defensive line would be left staring at Billy. The plan was perfect, but the execution was a failure. Billy got happy feet as he saw the defense blow past his lineman and decided that a scramble was in order. Two-yard loss.

"Block," Billy demanded.

"Dude, it's a screen pass." Scrub so-and-so was unphased by the beatdown.

"Billy, throw the damn ball!" Coach Selby was huffing as he arrived at the huddle. "We have gone over these plays a thousand times. You are the only QB out here this spring, but I will find somebody else if you won't run our plays. Now run it again!!!"

"OK, same play. On two, on two. Ready, Break."

"Blue forty-two, Blue forty-two! Readieee…..hut, hut."

Same play, loss of two. To Billy's defense, the scout team knew it was the same play and blew it up, shadowing the back and collapsing the pocket.

"Do we have anyone who can run this play? Anyone?" Coach Selby asked.

Cole raised his hand. "I'll try it, coach." He did not recognize that the question was rhetorical.

Coach McDonald looked at Coach Selby and shrugged his shoulders. "Couldn't be worse," he uttered so only the head coach could hear.

"Maybe this will light a fire under Billy's ass," Coach Selby responded. He directed his anger to number nineteen standing nearest him. "Go to the slot. Tell Cole to run the play at QB."

"Yes, sir."

Upon hearing the news, Billy threw his arms out to the side, palms up. "What?"

Coach Selby met him halfway. "Stand and watch a play. Maybe you'll learn something." And now for the scout team. "Stop trying to make the all-state scout team. In a real game, you won't know that play is coming so stop cheating. This is about running offense."

Cole repeated exactly what Billy had said in the huddle.

"OK, same play. On two, on two. Ready, Break."

"Blue forty-two, Blue forty-two! Readieee…..hut, hut." Same play, different result. The rush was fierce, but Cole stood in like a champ. He lobbed an adequate pass to his running back even knowing the hit was coming. In harmony, the O-line gracefully moved as one to the front of the ball carrier just as the ball arrived.

Seconds later Coach McDonald raised his arms and screamed, "Touchdown!"

Coach Selby turned to Billy, "See how easy that is? Okay, get in there and run the play again. Be patient and let the play develop this time."

Billy returned to the huddle. "Nineteen, you're out. Cole, back to the slot, and if you ever try that shit again, I'll fuck you up."

"OK, same play. On two, on two. Ready, Break," Billy said with more confidence. "Blue forty-two, Blue forty-two! Seeeeeet…..hut, hut."

Billy stood in the pocket awaiting the rush. He released the pass just a little too early to avoid the hit. The O-line had not yet shifted over before that catch was made. The back made a cut and one lineman managed a glancing block that allowed the back to pick up five yards."

"Better. Not great, but better. Billy, draw them in just a little more and let your linemen get over there."

"Got it, Coach."

Billy ran the huddle and the offense more productively from that day forward, but he was not yet ready to forget Cole's defection.

13

"Can I help you, sugar?" a plump woman asked from behind the register.

"I'm still deciding."

"Who's next, then?" It was a family with three little kids. Billy knew that it would take some time to serve them. The girl he wanted to talk to was finishing at the register and after loitering enough, he was next in line for the hot girl with the red hair. He had seen her in the halls of Foster Creek High School, but now he was standing in front of her.

When Mike Levy went to sea, Emily decided to take her first paycheck and do some serious self-care. Across the street from the commissary beside the Baskin-Robbins, a sign hung in the window. "Style, Cut, and Color from $39." Emily spent a week watching all the "befores and afters" from her front-row seat behind the ice cream counter. She would not go the DIY route again. She walked in on a Saturday morning as a redhead with straight, coarse hair, and walked out feeling like a supermodel. Her new auburn hair just kissed her shoulders. With hints of the red left behind, the stylist threw in some highlights a few shades lighter and she was a different woman. Fifteen days until her eighteenth birthday and seventy-two days from graduation, Emily was transformed.

She decided on a size smaller Baskin-Robbins shirt to accentuate the impact of the new Wonderbra. When she looked up and saw Billy, her knees nearly locked. She quickly recovered and she focused her large green eyes on Billy. Billy watched as her soft pink lips formed the words.

"Can I help you?"

God, she is so hot. Don't blow this, Billy. Think. Billy could only muster, "What do you recommend?"

This is unexpected. He's shy? But so cute. Play it cool, Emily.

"Try the gold medal ribbon. It's our best seller."

"Perfect, I'll take two scoops in a cup."

"For here or to go?" *Same either way, Stupid, Emily!!! Stupid.*

"For here, I think." Billy took note of the gaffe. "Can you join me?"

"I can't right now; I don't get a break for an hour," Emily said in an inviting tone.

"I'll wait." It was the only clever thing Billy had said all year.

She slowly bit at her lower right lip as she dipped the ice cream. She approached with the cup, then lowered her chin, and ran the play perfectly. As he reached for it, she brushed her face and moved her hair slightly as she answered, "OK. See you in an hour."

Billy and Emily flirted across the counter of the store for thirty minutes before the pasty lady whispered to Emily, "Sugar, don't make it *too* easy for him."

Emily would not take her advice. At 8:00 PM sharp, she walked to Billy. He did not take his eyes off her. He had used the hour to think about what he would say.

"I'm Billy McCaster."

"I'm Emily Levy. We met once before at your house in January. It's beautiful." *Why did I say that?*

"I can't believe I don't remember that. You are beautiful."

Her face was a little flush now. She tried to pivot. "Your mother hosted a tea for the wives and daughters of the new officers. She introduced you and mentioned your sister."

"Emma. She is at USC," Billy said.

"Right, Emma. You said quick hellos, got in your car, and left."

"Oh yeah, I'm never invited to those parties my mom throws. I drove around the corner to see my friend, Pete. I don't even remember what we did."

"Well, we had a great time. Your mother is so nice."

"Thank you, but she only does that out of duty." *Stupid, Billy!!!* "That came out wrong. Sorry."

"It's OK. I loved that tree in the front yard. I could sit on the lower branch for hours with a good book."

"How about a conversation with a good boy instead." *Smooth Billy.*

She blushed again and responded, "Depends on the boy."

"I'll pick you up tomorrow at 2:00," Billy said, playing it off like there was no option.

"Sure. I'll write down my address."

14

It was a perfect Sunday afternoon. Billy wore his best *Ralph Lauren Polo* oxford and *Calvin Klein* designer jeans. Emily pushed the season a little and decided on jeans and a sleeveless blouse, for which she emptied her account at the ATM just that morning.

Billy picked her up and had not yet made the connection between Emily and Cole. They arrived back at Billy's soon after and sat on the joggling board below the live oak as she had requested, although without a book in sight.

"Tell me about yourself, Emily. I want to know everything!" Billy laughed.

Emily giggled and almost blushed big time, but she pulled herself together. "Well, I was born in California on the Naval base in San Diego. I lived there until we moved to Indiana. I think I was ten."

Billy excitedly said, "I would love to live in California. I've always wanted to go."

"Maybe you can visit your sister in LA."

"My sister doesn't live in LA," Billy said, looking puzzled.

"I thought you said she went to USC."

"Oh, I get it now. She goes to the University of South Carolina. It's in Columbia, about two hours away, but she never comes home," Billy clarified.

"I should have known that. Do you want to go there, too?" Emily was doing reconnaissance now.

"Not sure. I hope to get a football scholarship to play somewhere. I kinda like Clemson a little better anyway."

"Is that in South Carolina too?" Emily began her dumb girl act.

"Don't let anybody outside of the base hear you say that. Yes, and they are bitter rivals."

"Gotcha. I have applied to IU. That's in Indiana," she said, disappointedly. She and Rob made a pact before they said their goodbyes on that last Sunday in Crane. It seemed stupid to her now. "Also at Charleston Southern. But I haven't decided for sure."

"You've already applied? Are you a senior? How old are you?" Billy's expression was alarming. He knew he had to be careful now.

"How old are *you?*" Emily asked.

Billy thought about lying for a moment. "I'm seventeen. Well, I will be in a couple of weeks."

"I'm seventeen too," Emily said. She was not discouraged. *God, he's cute.* "And I'm a senior. You?"

Billy wanted to gloss over the subject. He dismissively responded, "Well, we're the same age, so it shouldn't matter, but I'm a junior."

Billy was relieved when she agreed. After half an hour, Cookie McCaster popped her head out of the front door.

"Billy, I have to run an errand for your dad. I should be back in about an hour. Be nice to that lovely girl."

"OK, Mom."

Minutes later, Cookie drove away. As he waved goodbye, Billy suggested they go in and have some tea.

"Sure, I need to get out of the sun anyway." Emily was starting to pink up but the fact of the matter was that she was a little cold. They dismounted the joggling board as a gentle breeze blew some of the lingering Spanish moss across her hair.

Emily returned to her dumb girl routine and asked, "What is this stuff anyway? It looks like a beard on a yard gnome."

Billy laughed, and it was just the response she wanted. She had learned that her best flirt was to act a little dumb and let the boy rescue her from her own stupidity. It seemed to work on Billy.

Billy's smile widened and he said, "You're funny. It's Spanish moss."

As they reached the kitchen entrance, Billy opened the door like a true Southern gentleman. As Emily entered, she rubbed her arms and shivered slightly. Billy took it as an invitation to touch her.

"Are you cold?" Billy reached for her arms and gently rubbed them to warm her up. "Is that better?" he said with an empathetic tone.

She turned around to address him and found herself pleasantly close to him. She softly responded, "Yes. That feels nice."

His hands caressed her arms and then found her hands. It was all new to Billy. It was not something he planned or practiced, and it was moving fast.

Emily continued, "You have strong hands, Billy."

Billy understood; she was signaling him, and he moved her hands to his neck. He returned his empty hands to her waist. He leaned forward, and she leaned in. Billy gave her a quick, awkward kiss. Emily pulled him back in for more. Billy's hands moved slightly lower from her waist to the upper curve of her hips. After a longer, more passionate kiss, he mustered up the nerve to ask, "Do you want to go to my room?"

Emily knew what it meant. She remembered how much she liked sex with her lifeguard in Crane. It already felt different with Billy. She felt drawn to him. She thought *'Could love happen this fast?'* Perhaps it was the neglect at home that spawned her need to feel loved. She knew her mom would not approve and that was the tipping point for her. She whispered in his ear, "I'd like that." She kissed him one more time and moved her warm hand from his head around his neck and brushed his chest with her fingers. She left no doubt as to her intent.

Billy was in a state outside of himself not knowing exactly what to do. The two were lost in the moment and too far gone to turn back now. Each was guided by a sudden and uncontrollable desire. She raised her eyebrows, tilted her head, smiled, and gave a slight nod. Billy took her hand and guided her upstairs. She returned her hand to his chest and helped him remove his shirt. To Emily, Billy was the most handsome boy that she had ever met. Billy was taken in by Emily's smile and perfect skin. He slowly moved his hands up her waist and under her blouse, She pulled her blouse over her head, and he fell into her breasts. They removed the rest of their clothes and laid naked together on the bed. Billy kissed her while they explored each other. They were swept away in the emotions of the act.

They both felt the specialness of what they had shared, but Billy was lost for words. Nothing was said for the longest time as Billy held Emily. He did not expect to be so consumed by it all, and that feeling lingered for the longest time. Emily had had sex before, but this was different. With her lifeguard, she was left feeling a little broken. Billy had made her feel whole. This was the first time she made love. She was in deep love with Billy.

After an eternity of awkward silence, Billy finally whispered, "I love you, Emily Levy."

She took her head off his chest and turned to him saying, "I love you, too."

They both needed more time to digest what they had both said and heard. After more silence, Billy realized their time was fading. "I could stay here all day but my mom will probably be back soon. We better get downstairs."

They dressed and made it back downstairs just in time to pour the promised glass of tea when Cookie walked in from the garage. Cookie knew the kids had been making out as neither looked as together as when she left. "Billy, your father needs you to meet him to run an errand. He said it might take a couple of hours and to wear some old clothes."

"What is it?" Billy asked.

Cookie recovered quickly, "I don't know, he just said he would be here in a little while."

"I should go home soon," Emily said as she tried to disguise her disappointment.

Billy said, "Well, tell Dad I'll be right back. I'm going to take Emily home."

Cookie had not recognized Emily from a distance in the yard, but she knew exactly who she was when she encountered her in the kitchen. She remembered her as the daughter of that lady who showed up nearly drunk at her tea party. Cookie sized her up as low class and would tell Billy as much when he returned. She hoped it had not already gone too far. "Be careful, but hurry back."

Billy drove slowly, wanting to milk every second of the day. It was his best day ever. As he arrived at Emily's house, his tone changed.

Billy said, "What's Cole doing here?" He finally made the connection. "Wait, is he…"

Emily interrupted, "He's my brother."

15

Pete Dillard was quick to latch on to Billy in middle school. They lived near each other on base from middle through high school. In the Navy, it was unusual for friends to stick around for that long. As others moved away and as the shine on Billy's star began to fade over time, Pete remained a loyal friend. Billy's following got smaller each year. He constantly belittled his classmates. He was no better on a court or athletic field. His inflated ego took a hit when some of the boys grew stronger, taller, and more coordinated. Pete was still Billy's dim-bulbed lapdog as spring football practice wound down.

Cole turned out to be a dependable and likable friend to his new teammates. Pete was no exception. Billy was still a little chilly but willing to make an effort with Cole for Emily's sake. He enlisted Pete to ask Cole to go fishing one day after school. After Cole agreed, the plan was for Billy to casually bump into them where Pete would say, "Hey Billy, Cole and me are goin' fishin' tomorrow after school. Wanna go?" Surprisingly, given the lack of practice, Pete ran the play well.

"Sounds like fun. Is it OK with you if I tag along, Cole?"

Not Re♦ or scrub. Cole. Who is this? Can I really trust Billy of all people? "Sure. Sounds like a good time. I didn't know you liked to fish."

"Oh yeah. Pete and I fish all the time," Billy lied like a sack of potatoes. He and Pete had never fished, but Pete's garage had some old rods and lures left behind by the last Navy brats. Emily was always talking up Cole and told Billy about the boat and the afternoons spent on the lake with their dad back in Crane. He and Pete doubted Cole would accept an invitation to join them on base for a round of golf, so they hatched out a plan for fishing. Cole fished the brackish waters for redfish, Pete was just going through the motions. Billy was fishing for Cole.

Sitting along the banks of the tidal creek, Billy began to see Cole in a different light. "He's a lot like Emily when you can get him to talk," he said in the direction of Pete.

"Thanks, I think."

"You are a man of few words, Cole Levy. We need to do this again one day."

"Alright."

"Do you like to play golf?" Dim-bulb said, earning an *"Are you stupid?"* look from Billy.

"I like fishing, hiking, hunting...those kinda things."

"You ever hunted snipe?" This time Billy gave Pete a nod of approval. Billy justified this as an initiation. He gave Pete another look that clearly said *"I'll take it from here."*

"What's a snipe? Do you shoot it or trap it?"

It was the first nibble Billy had received all day. "It's a bird that lives near the marsh. It runs really fast, kinda like a roadrunner."

"I saw one of those at a zoo when I was a kid. Seems like it would be hard to hunt. What do you do with it after you get it, eat it?"

"No dude, catch and release, just like fish. We hunt it just for the sport. It's a stupid bird and gets trapped pretty easily, just need a little patience–hey, we can take you next Saturday night if you want."

"Night?"

"Yeah, its vision is worse at night."

"Yeah, he's blind at night!"

Shut up, Pete. "Not actually blind, kinda legally blind, maybe."

"I see. All we have is a shotgun. My mom is going away for the weekend and leaving Emily in charge, but I can sneak it out."

Billy noted that Emily would be home alone. It was the first week of April now, and it had been weeks since he and Emily first made love. If he played it right, he could get Pete to help keep Cole *hunting* for a couple of hours. Billy and Emily found their first time in his bed much more fun than the back seat of his car. Maybe they could use Emily's room. Maybe he could even stay the night. He would just need to get Cole to agree to it. "You won't need a gun or knife or anything like that. You are supposed to use a net, but we use a big piece of burlap, and that always works fine."

"Yeah, a burlap bag." Pete insisted on participating.

"It's hard to describe, but you do have to have a way to close up the burlap after you get the snipe." Billy covered for Pete.

"Kinda like a drawstring or something?"

"Exactly like a drawstring, Cole." Billy could only begin to imagine how he and Pete were going to make that. *Idiot, Thanks for nothing, Pete.*

"Well, it sounds fun. Will I need anything?"

"Just a flashlight. Maybe we can camp afterward or stay over at somebody's house. My mom is having some stupid tea so we can't stay there. Well..."

Before Billy could think of a way to pivot from Pete's house, Cole volunteered. "It's just me and Emily so you can stay over at my house."

"It's a plan then. Let's not tell anybody what we're doin." *We'll have half the team going with us if we're not careful. It'll be more fun with just us. More snipe for us too.*

"You'll have to teach me how to do it."

Teach you we will, my young Jedi. "It's easy. We'll show you Saturday."

It was Thursday evening. Billy and Cole both had trouble sleeping that night. Cole thought of what it would be like to catch the snipe, but Billy's thoughts were of Emily. As usual, Pete had no thoughts.

Billy had Pete on lock-down. "Not a word to anyone Pete. I mean it. Don't fuck this up!!!" Pete went all of Friday and didn't say anything. Cole almost slipped up once. In homeroom, he asked Mr. Jaymes, "Mr. Jaymes, you know what a snipe is?"

"It's a bird that lives in the marsh. But.."

The bell rang, and Cole cut him off.

As Cole was trying to leave, Mr. Jaymes quietly asked "Why do you ask, Cole?

"Well, it's a secret but Billy and Pete are taking me on a snipe hunt tomorrow night."

"Billy?"

"Yeah, Billy McCaster. Do you know him?"

"Yes, good kid." Had it been anyone but Billy, Mr. Jaymes would have instantly spilled the beans. His delay gave Cole enough time to scurry down the hall and disappear into a mass of bodies. He could not wait until Monday to hear all about it.

He would not have to wait that long.

16

Ann Levy and her friends were not invited to Cookie's party. The Sunset Ladies Auxiliary had their own plans. Ann had learned long ago that there were two types of officers' wives, and she and Cookie were on opposite sides of the ledger. Having correctly sized Cookie up at the January tea, Ann found Cookie aloof and artificial. Her pack agreed. Cookie looked down on the women that lived off the main base and the ladies of the Auxiliary knew it.

Ann left final instructions for Emily before they left on Saturday. By the time Emily got home from work and saw the note, Cole had already marked out the first part of #1.

1. ~~Make sure you know where Cole is. Both of you need to be home by 11 each night. I WILL call.~~
2. Keep the house clean.
3. I am at the Lodge Alley Inn. I can be home in 45 minutes. The number is taped to the phone.

I'll be home Monday morning. It's a parent conference morning so you and Cole don't have school until 10. Love you, Mom. PS. Got your report cards in the mail today before I left. Proud of you both.

The Charleston peninsula has several unique, eclectic areas. The area around East Bay to King Street and from Market Street to Broad Street contained hundreds of restaurants, bars, and clubs. The Lodge

Alley Inn is a quaint lodge tucked away in a brick-lined alley with a large courtyard.

It was moved and seconded that the ladies would need to eat first. They wanted seafood, so they checked the map and decided on AW Shucks, around the corner off Queen Street. AW Shucks had great reviews and was known for the seafood, especially the oysters. The ladies chose it for its name: *A.W. Shucks Oyster Bar*, with emphasis on the BAR.

To their surprise, the ladies were told there was only a short wait for dinner so they started in the bar. Round one was a Long Island Iced Tea. Sticker shock set in when the drinks were nearly ten dollars each. It was explained that the drinks contained four mini bottles–gin, vodka, white rum, and tequila. Add the triple sec and a little Coke and that made for an expensive drink. The ladies weren't lightweights. They had stamina from practicing their sport so frequently, and the four-shot drink simply gave them a very light buzz. The buzzer in Wanda's hand went off and the party was seated for dinner. This time, they took advantage of a two-for-one special and ordered tequila shots. Dinner was consumed quickly by tourist standards, and the ladies asked for the check, hurriedly paid, and then left, anxious to start their pub crawl.

They scarcely had to walk past more than two buildings before they found another interesting historical site, that is to say, a bar. Drinks and more drinks. Now the ladies were on their way to being more than a little buzzed. Ann appeared to be beyond that. Janet had been keeping score and surmised that Ann was having three drinks for every one of theirs and she was getting out of control. She was loud and wobbly, and her words were getting a little slurred, and often what she said didn't make sense. She became obnoxiously drunk. Men began taking notice of the pack. To keep her out of trouble, Janet appointed herself as chief executive and said, " Ann, you may want to slow down a little bit."

"You shoun like my husband. Don't shudge me!" Ann's retort was quick, loud, and sharp. The other ladies looked at Janet and they all rolled their eyes. Ann did not notice as she was looking elsewhere. She was particularly flattered when a very handsome used-car salesman type approached her with an offer to buy her a drink.

"That is very nice. Thank you," Ann flirtingly replied. She uttered barely understandable quips to the man and waved her hands awkwardly as she talked. The man noticed her wedding ring.

"I see you are married."

Ann avoided answering his question. "Are you married?"

"No, I'm divorced. With two kids." He figured this would not go anywhere.

"Well, I am married, but I am not married tonight. Do you know what I mean?" as she winked and pursed her lips trying to be as sexy as she was capable given her induced condition. She leaned in and whispered in his ear, "Do you want to get out of here?"

For the rest of the Sunset Social Club, the party ended at 1:00 AM with a walk past the now well-lit fountain in the courtyard. Ann Levy missed the first night at The Lodge Alley Inn, seducing Carl, her strikingly handsome used-car salesman from Charleston. It would be the second time she had been unfaithful to her husband, both times a result of too much liquor.

The next morning, she awoke and looked over at her 'hunk,' a heavy, leather-faced frog. Although she could not remember exactly everything they did, she knew she had sex with him, although she simply couldn't remember if it was good sex or bad sex. She would never remember that she had, in fact, had him twice. *Oh shit, Ann! Why, why, why???*

"You OK, darlin'?" Frog Face asked. He began to reach for her, hoping to get laid while she was sober.

She was dismissive and found him gross. He smelled and the bedroom was nasty. And she did not know where they were. "I need to get back to my friends." *I don't even remember your name.*

"Sure thing. How about a little breakfast first."

Well, that's the least he could do. "That would be nice."

"Yes, it would. Eggs and bacon are in the fridge and the pans are in the bottom of the stove. I'll grab a quick shower then meet you in the kitchen. After we eat, I'll run you back over. It's just twenty minutes away."

Ass Hole! Oh God, please don't let me be near Foster Creek.

The trip from west of the Ashley River only took fifteen minutes in the absence of traffic on Sunday morning. After the shower, Ann found him less offensive than when she awoke finding him stinky and naked beside her. *Why do slightly heavy men always look better when they are standing up? Maybe I should talk to him a bit more.* Fortunately, Froggy barely came to a complete stop to let her out on the road. She gave him an awkward smile and glance to thank him and let him know that she thought he was a piece of shit. He did not reciprocate.

She walked through the narrow alley past the valet stand before she reached the courtyard. As she appeared she heard the catcalls from the ladies on the balcony. She worked to hide the shame expressed on her face. *They did not see him.* She still had plausible deniability.

"Missed you last night" the platinum blonde with black roots yelled from the balcony.

"Sorry, I wished I had stayed here. Nothing happened, I threw up on his carpet then I just passed out on a couch."

The ladies on the balcony gave her a courtesy nod. When she disappeared into the stairwell, one of them said "She looks like he rode her all night." The gossip and whispering continued long after the girls returned home Sunday evening, cutting their trip short by a night after a little too much partying on night one.

Ann had missed the night at the Inn. She would later learn that she missed something far more important.

17

Billy and Emily spent Friday's lunch devising a workable Saturday night plan. At dusk, Billy would pick up Pete and Cole and take them to the marshlands behind the school. Cole would have the honor of catching the first snipe. Billy would get Pete settled to keep an eye on Cole. Billy would then slip back to the house for round one with Emily. He would check back to find Cole where he left him, preaching patience. He would then pick Pete up and take him back to the base. He would return to Emily and wait for Cole to walk home, empty snipe bag in hand.

When Billy picked him up, Pete explained that he had to be home by 9:00 PM. He was semi-grounded for doing poorly on his 3rd quarter report card. He was only able to go out on the pretense that he was going to the school for some mythical extra credit project. His mom insisted that she would pick him up in front of the school at 9:00 PM. Billy reexamined his timeline and concluded no alterations to the plan were necessary. "So I don't even have to take you back home?" he suddenly realized his luck.

The boys arrived at Cole's with flashlights and a tarp that had haphazardly been stitched to resemble a large bag. "Get in the back, Pete!"

"But I called shotgun."

"No, you didn't. Just get in the back." As Cole approached the car, Pete rolled over the front seat into the back. Billy rolled his eyes and directed his attention toward Cole. "Hey man, ready to get some snipe?"

"Yeah."

"Well, don't be *too* excited."

Cole smiled and Billy chose to ignore the gap.

"Where are we goin'?"

"Just over to the marsh behind the school."

It was only a quarter mile to the school and Cole thought it silly that Billy needed to drive. Soon after, Billy parked in front of the school and popped the hatch to his silver Z. Pete was wedged in what was generously labeled a back seat and after a tug from Cole, he was out. The two met Billy at the back of the car as Billy was pulling out the craft project.

"I thought it was burlap. That's a tarp."

"Pete's mom threw away our other one last month, so we had to make this. We didn't have time to get a new snipe bag from the Navy Exchange." Billy thought that the Navy Exchange added a touch of legitimacy.

"Oh," Cole was now on the hook.

As the boys walked around the school, Billy began to explain how the hunt worked. Cole would hold the bag, positioned near the small isolated pine tree nearest the marsh, about a quarter mile northeast of the stadium. "We'll go to the other side of that grove of trees where the marsh bends and start looking for the snipe. As they come out of the marsh, Pete and I will surround 'em and cut 'em off and funnel 'em your way. You will turn on your flashlight. The snipe will be attracted to the light. We'll drive 'em toward you and when they run by, throw your bag over one and then yell for us. Keep quiet until you get one, we don't want to spook them. One more thing, be patient. They don't always come out of the marsh when it first gets dark. Sometimes it takes a while. You'll hear us making a racket when we see 'em so get that flashlight ready cause you'll know they're coming. After you get the first one, I'll take a turn holding the bag, and Pete can show you how to corral 'em."

Cole was still picturing how it all worked when Billy and Pete disappeared through the darkness of the tree line. Billy positioned Pete where he could see Cole. "Don't move. If he figures this out before I come back, just keep him here. I'll try to get back before you leave."

With that, Billy circled the treeline and doubled back to his car. He sped back to Emily. She was waiting for him, wearing nothing but one of her father's white formal wing collar shirts.

"Now that's sexy."

He didn't remember taking the required steps to reach her. They fell into each other, kissed, and soon after, she led him to her bed. At exactly 8:30 PM, Billy returned as planned. He found Pete, and they went to check on Cole. Cole was a patient outdoorsman, and, as expected, the boys found him leaning against the tree. "Do you want to switch off?" Billy asked.

Cole was reassured at the sight of the boys. "No, I'm good. Have you seen any yet?"

Pete chimed in, "We heard 'em. I think they leave the marsh to lay their eggs to keep snakes and stuff from eating them. Good darkness tonight, so they oughta be out soon."

Somehow Pete's explanation made sense. "I can stay all night if I need to." In reality, Cole thought maybe another hour or two at most.

The boys confirmed their commitment and soon disappeared into the darkness before they reached the woods. Billy led Pete through the woods back around to the front of the school.

"8:50. Just in time." With that, Billy got into his car. As he pulled out of the lot, he saw the headlights arrive where he left Pete. Now that Pete was safely delivered, his thoughts returned to Emily.

18

Pete's mother waited for over an hour at the school before she went home. She thought out loud, "He better be there." She arrived home and waited until 11:00 PM before she decided to call Cookie.

Cookie was finishing the dishes from the party when the phone rang in the McCaster's kitchen. "Hello."

"Cookie, it's Laura. Is Pete over there with Billy?"

"No, I had another one of the awful welcoming parties and he told me he was spending the night with Pete."

"Well, they're not here. These boys---wait, I think this might be him now," she said, having heard a single car door shut.

Pete knew he couldn't sneak in and he failed to think about the consequences of his actions. He instantly recognized that look on his mother's face.

"Where have you been? I was at the school and I waited for over an hour. I was worried sick. Who was that in the car?"

"Billy dropped me off."

"Your father is still at some official event but when he gets home later I will discuss this with him and we will decide on further punishment. Go to your room and we will talk to you tomorrow morning. You're grounded at least until school is out."

Pete heard his mother say she would wait until his father got home to discuss it. Pete thought this was a positive sign because his father was always a little more lenient; especially for a military officer. He decided to challenge the statement, "But..."

"No. Say nothing. NOTHING!!"

He followed orders and went to his room. Laura sat for a few minutes and poured herself a shot of tequila. She was sipping at her third shot and a quick minute later, the nerves had just settled when she was startled by the phone. "*Who on earth is calling at 11:30 at night?*"

"Laura, it's Cookie. I just wanted to check that Billy was there with Pete."

"Billy dropped Pete off probableeeeeee 30 minutes ago? Then left."

"Well, he's not home and he's not there, so could you ask Pete if he knows where he is?"

"PEEEEETE! GET IN HERE! Where is Billy?"

Mumble, mumble, mumble. Laura was fluent in Pete's mumble and returned to the phone, "Cookie, something's not right. I'll call you right back."

After fifteen minutes of grilling, Pete surrendered. Some friends drove by and saw him waiting in the parking lot and asked him if he wanted to go party with them. He left out most of the details, but was quick to dish out the dirt on Billy's whereabouts, hoping to pivot his mom to a different target. Utterly defeated, Pete returned to his room.

The phone rang again in the McCaster's kitchen. "Laura?"

"Cookie, it's me. Billy is over spending the night with some boy named Cole Levy, over near the high school. Pete had planned to go, too, but I grounded him this morning before he could ask permission."

"Does Pete know where he lives?" She thought for a second to let it go. She always had a blindspot for Billy. "Nevermind, I'll just wait until tomorrow morning and deal with him then."

"Well, he doesn't know the exact address, but said it was on Sunset. And Laura, the boys are there with an older sister, Emily. The dad is still out on a sub and the mom is gone for the weekend."

"I better go try to find him then."

"Sorry, Cookie."

"Not your fault, Laura. I may need to call you tomorrow."

"Certainly. Be careful." Laura knew that Cookie's parties involved proper social drinks. She worried that Cookie might have had a few more after everybody left.

"Thanks. Bye."

19

Cookie drove around the last curve on Sunset when she saw Billy's car. She thought it looked out of place on the property. She thought briefly that Commander McCaster would shit his pants if he knew Billy had lied. She also thought that if Billy's car was taken away for any time whatsoever, she would have to drive him around. She decided before she even put the car in park that the Commander would not need to know about this. She parked on the street and approached the front door. As she neared the door, she noticed Emily through a narrow gap in the blinds. She was now wearing a camo T-shirt that barely covered her buttocks. She recognized it as the very same one Billy picked out at the Navy Exchange that morning. It was seconds before Billy appeared shirtless and wrapped his arms around her. She pounded on the door.

It was midnight. Billy and Emily had lost track of time when they heard the angry strikes on the door. "Oh shit, Emily. I forgot about Cole. He sounds pissed. I'll get it. You better get dressed."

She took off her T-shirt and handed it to him. He wanted to just stare but the rumbling on the door broke his trance. He slipped on the shirt and waited until Emily shut the door to her room before he unlocked the deadbolt.

As he opened the door, his mother heard him say, "Cole, I'm so…Mom, what are you doing here?"

"Get in your car now. I am not doing this here."

"Mom, I need to do something first."

"I know what's going on here. I just hope you've not been stupid!"

"Love is not stupid, Mom."

"LOVE?! You are stupid. That girl has her claws in you. In the car now." Emily appeared from her room expecting to see Cole. "Not a word from you, young lady. I remember you and that drunk mother of yours now. Stay away from my son. Billy, go get in the car. Go straight home. I am right behind you."

As Billy turned to Emily, he saw tears falling off her cheeks. He mouthed "I'm sorry. I love you."

"Now, Billy!" Cookie was even more forceful now as she pointed to the car.

Billy did not remember the drive home. He thought of Emily. He thought of how angry his dad would be. Finally, he worried about Cole.

20

March 29, 1988

Cole wept as he saw Mr. Jaymes approaching. He was hoping for an expeditious ending and significant kindness. Neither was Mr. Jaymes' reality.

"Snipe hunt? Billy, Billy, Billy."

"Do you have a way to cut me loose?" Cole pleaded.

"Where are your clothes?" Alan Jaymes asked, still failing to get that this was more than a funny joke.

"They're just over there." Cole nodded toward the clothes, expecting Alan Jaymes to fetch them first and cover him up.

Instead, Mr. Jaymes looked around the tree and told Cole that he would have to stand up for him to get to the tape. Cole was more than capable of standing up himself but Mr. Jaymes would not miss his opportunity to touch the boy. He grabbed lower than around the waist and when upright, he brushed Cole's chest with his hand and then slid it to his shoulder.

"What are you doing!?" Cole demanded.

Mr. Jaymes then noticed the blue paint on Cole's genitals. He removed a handkerchief from his suit pocket and moved it toward Cole's stomach.

"Stop. Cut me down and don't touch me again."

"Cole, I would never. I'm just trying to help you."

With that, Mr. Jaymes stopped and after a final look, he went to the back of the tree, produced a pocket knife from his slacks, and cut Cole's hands loose. Cole quickly leaned down and ripped away the duct tape that fused his ankles. From there, he rose only to see Mr. Jaymes staring at the blue paint. Cole moved his hands to shield his blue genitalia from the man's gaze, pulled up his jeans, and ran to his shoes and the rest of his clothes. He glanced back and took notice of Mr. Jaymes still fixated on his body. He took a deep breath and let out a long sigh as he shook his head from side to side. The paint had dried. He slipped on his shoes, pulled his T-shirt over his head, and picked up his shirt and socks. As he turned to run away he found it necessary to muster the courage to face Mr. Jaymes one last time. "Please don't tell anyone about this."

"Oh, I won't. If you need to talk about what happened or anything, come see me at school."

Cole never wanted to see Mr. Jaymes again. He never wanted to see anyone again. "*Screw Billy. Screw Pete.*" Cole hatched a thousand plans on his run home. He was in a clear state of panic when he ran into the house and found Emily staring at the wall.

"Where have you been?" she said. Emily appeared disheveled in the same clothes from the night before, and she had clearly not slept.

Cole answered abruptly, "Nowhere!" He went directly to the bathroom and locked the door. Seconds later as Emily leaned her ear to the bathroom door. She thought she heard crying. The sound of the shower registered before she was sure.

21

After an 11:00 AM checkout, the ladies loaded the car and decided to take in some of the more traditional sites. The auxiliary wanted nothing to do with alcohol that morning. They tried to order a Bloody Mary just to get over the hangover, but the waitress at Poogan's Porch explained a Sunday in Charleston was dry unless at a private club. The ladies enjoyed a leisurely lunch of the house specialty, Southern vittles. They walked off their lunch on King Street and spent time browsing through the craftsman's stalls at the Charleston City Market. Ann convinced herself that the visit to St. Philip's Episcopal Church, built in 1838 on Church Street adjacent to the slave market, was less about an interest in history and more about her salvation. The girls climbed into the minivan around 5:00 PM and started home. The soon-to-be former Sunset Ladies' Drinking Club permanently adjourned when they arrived home nearly half an hour later.

As she entered the house Ann knew that something was amiss. The tension was like static lightning in the air. It was simply too quiet. Emily was asleep on the couch, which was unusual in itself, and Cole was nowhere to be found. The door shut and Emily awoke. "Mom where have you been!? I tried to call you, and you didn't answer the phone."

"I told you I would be at The Lodge Alley Inn in Charleston for the weekend. I'm even back a night early. When did you try to call me and what did you want?"

"Last night at about midnight. Something happened and Cole didn't come home. I was worried and upset and I needed you. Nobody answered the phone. Nobody. I called again and again and finally, an hour later, some lady answered. She sounded drunk and I could barely understand her. I asked if you were there and she said you weren't back in yet. Mom, that was at 1:00 in the morning. Besides, you said you would call us, and you didn't." *Clearly I hadn't planned on you calling. Truth be told, I was counting on you NOT calling."*

"Did you try to call again?" What a relief when Emily answered no. "Well, I got in shortly after that," she lied. "So what is going on with Cole?"

"You just need to go talk to him. He's been in his room all day and he won't talk to me. I think something bad has happened. He's not hurt or anything, but something's wrong. Really wrong."

"You don't look so good yourself. Did something happen to you, too?"

"I'm just tired. You need to talk to Cole first. I can wait." *I'm not ready to talk to you about Billy. I'm not ready to talk to you about his mother barging in on us, practically naked in* **your** *kitchen. I'm not ready to talk to you about how I ignored your directions; how I didn't care about where Cole was, how I only thought about myself. I'm not ready to talk about my part in the snipe hunt plan. I don't know what went wrong with Cole. I'm scared and we need Dad. And I'm not ready to tell you that I may be pregnant with Billy McCaster's baby.*

Ann Levy unsuccessfully spent the next few hours trying to lure Cole out of his room. The night passed with no time to sleep. Their demons stole it. Ann thought of how she failed them. She felt extreme guilt that she chose to fuck Froggy instead of being there for her kids. She was afraid to shut her bedroom door, afraid she would miss Cole.

Emily heard her sobs even over her own. Her thoughts were of Billy and the last thing his mother had said to her. She fretted over how she might not see him again and of her error in judgment that first time at Billy's house.

Cole relived the nightmare. He thought of what Billy and Pete did to him. He thought of how they wanted to humiliate him. He wondered why he still could not remember all of the details. He remembered seeing the blue paint but he didn't remember when Billy did it. He remembered every detail about Mr. Jaymes, and he sobbed. Their demons crippled all the Levys that night, robbing them of both sleep and their innocence.

The next morning, Ann made multiple attempts to wake up Cole. Finally, under the threat of breaking the door down, she heard angry words from the other side of the door. "I'm not going to school today, I don't feel well."

"Cole!" Ann was desperate to get him to school. She needed a drink to steady herself.

"I don't feel well, please leave me alone." There was a finality in the sharp retort.

Emily was eager to get to school. She needed to see Billy. She needed to hold him again. She needed to touch him to exercise her advantage over his mother. She needed him to take away the pain that Mrs. McCaster had so easily doled out. She needed Billy to choose her. She could barely think of anything else.

Cole scarcely left his room. He had no appetite. His mother got only an occasional glimpse of him when he went to the bathroom. His blue eyes were red from the tears and her disheveled son would still not talk. The drama with Cole spilled over to Tuesday and then Wednesday.

Ann was a detached mom, anxious to return to her private time with the bottle, but even the worst parents ache when their kids hurt. This was also true of Ann Levy. By Wednesday morning, serious withdrawal set in. Her hands shook as she reached for the phone to call the principal of Foster Creek High School.

22

Ann Levy only went to Cole's schools twice in her life. She did not attend PTA meetings, sporting events, or open houses. After Cole didn't make the basketball team in Crane, even a detached Ann Levy could gauge the depression in her son. She called the principal of Loogootee High and explained Cole's state of mind. She was worried. She tried to explain that Cole was sick during tryouts. He had an off day, if he could just have another chance. Finally, she took a rare, more cognitive approach.

"Listen, the team doesn't need Cole. I know that. Basketball doesn't need Cole, but Cole needs basketball. He doesn't make friends easily. He needs this for his self-esteem."

"Ma'am, I do understand but I can't tell a coach which players to keep."

"Just let me talk to the Coach. Please. I just need to have peace of mind that I've done everything for my son. I need to understand how to help him through this. He's so distraught. Please."

"Well, I will have to ask Coach if he'll take a meeting with you. I'll have to call you back."

"Oh, thank you so much. When do you think I will hear back from you?"

"Well ma'am, it might be later today before I can catch him. He has 7th-period planning. After that, he monitors the buses, so I know I can catch him then. He has about half an hour after duty before practice and practice lasts around an hour and a half. I will call you either way…OK…" He was opening the office door as he was talking. Ann Levy thanked him and left.

Ann got a call later that afternoon confirming an appointment with the coach for the next day at 1:15 PM in his office behind the gym. Ann arrived early and a student office worker escorted her to the coach's office. She thanked the student and turned toward the coach.

"I'm Mrs. Levy, Cole's mom. Thank you so much for seeing me."

"Yes ma'am, you're welcome. Please have a seat. Now how can I help you?"

Ann had a few extra sips of courage before she came. She hoped Coach Hooper didn't notice. She sat down in the chair and looked up. What she instantly noticed was how handsome the coach was. He was tall, of course, and trim. He sat against his desk in loose sweatpants and a tight, compression-fit shirt. Anne got caught looking him over. She tried to recover.

"Well, I just wanted to talk about Cole a little. I know he is not the greatest basketball player in the world…"

Not even close.

"…but it would mean the world to him to be part of the team. Is there anything he can do to change your mind?"

"We've already started practice and carved out roles for our boys. It really would be unfair to the rest of the team to start over. I am sorry."

She half-listened. Her attention slowly changed from Cole to Coach Hooper's chest. She was caught looking again when she said "I'll do anything. ANYTHING!"

The coach paused for a moment and registered what her eyes were saying. It wasn't the first time that a lonely mom had thought to prostitute herself. He had a rehearsed response that let a woman leave with her dignity. Before he could deliver his spiel, Ann's hands were pulling at the drawstring around his sweatpants. The knot loosened and the pants slipped down a little and the top of his briefs were exposed. He had never let this happen before. Her fingertips hung on the elastic like a wet towel hangs on a clothesline. He felt her hands on his skin. He could not mistake her intent.

"Mrs. Levy, this won't change anything."

She felt a swell as she pulled his underwear down over his sweats, "It doesn't matter now." The door was shut just in time as the athletic secretary returned to her desk.

Several minutes passed, then the office door opened and a fully clothed Coach Hooper was surprised at the presence of Mrs. Gilbert. Ann emerged and asked her for something to drink, "a Coke perhaps."

Coach replied, "We don't have any here, Mrs. Levy, but there is a machine in the front lobby. Thank you for coming in. Tell Cole to try again next year." He tried to be coy but Mrs. Gilbert quickly sized up the situation. She wished it had been her.

Her visit to Foster Creek High would be different. The visit was to attain information rather than persuasion. The past Saturday in Charleston left fresh wounds and she was not remotely interested in a repeat of Mr. Hooper. Cole had stayed home for the third day in a row. He had only missed one day of school in the previous nine years.

"Hello Principal Wade. Thank you for seeing me."

"How may I help you, Mrs. Levy? Our football coaches sure do think a lot of Cole."

"Thank you. He loves being part of the team, and he did so well last quarter, but something has happened, and he hasn't given me any details. He hasn't been to school since last week, and I don't think he's physically ill. I've never seen him like this."

"Hmmm. Cole is fitting in well here, and we don't want to see him take a step backward. What has he told you?"

"Well, it all started last Saturday night. He was out all night and neither he nor his sister will tell me who with. *I am not telling you about what I did Saturday night!* Finally last night, he mumbled something about a Mr. Jaymes."

"What about Mr. Jaymes?" *Of course, it has to involve that idiot. I am fed up with him. I hope he's fucked up so badly this time that I have to fire his ass.*

"Cole said Mr. Jaymes found him Sunday morning, and I should talk to him."

Mr. Wade was on the intercom to his secretary. "Barb, find a teacher to go cover Mr. Jaymes' class and tell him to come to my office." Five minutes later, Mr. Jaymes was in the principal's office. As he sat down it seemed too familiar. Mr. Wade introduced Mrs. Levy.

"Alan, this is Mrs. Levy, Cole's mother."

He extended his hand. "Mrs. Levy, happy to meet you. *Oh shit. Oh shit. He told her everything.*" When she shook his hand and half smiled, he felt a slight improvement in his gut.

Mr. Wade then filled Alan in on everything he knew. He packaged it in a way that let Alan somehow know that he better tell everything he knows. Alan's hands were wet and he wiped them on his pants. Mr. Wade took notice. This was not his first rodeo. He knew from experience when kids or teachers started fidgeting, matters often ended badly. In a shaky voice, Alan began to spin his version of the facts.

"You know I open the auditorium on Sunday morning for church, right? Last Sunday when I drove up, Cole was against a tree in the wooded area past the far side of the parking lot, and he was naked." Alan registered the looks of shock on the faces of his audience. He thought perhaps he should not have opened with that. "He saw it was me and screamed for help. I ran as fast as I could to get him. His hands were taped behind a tree...and his pants were below his taped ankles," a gasp from Mrs. Levy this time, "... so I cut him loose with my pocket knife and helped him find his shoes and shirt. He said somebody had painted his genital area blue as a joke and tied him up. He told me to look at what they did. I was uncomfortable staring at him like that but he insisted. I offered him my handkerchief to clean it off, but he said he just wanted to go home and forget about the whole thing. I waited until he got dressed and made sure he was OK. He asked me not to say anything. It didn't seem like a big deal to him, more like innocent fun. I was the first person at the school, or I guess church, and I'm pretty sure nobody saw him from the road because it was still a little foggy."

"Why didn't you report this on Monday? It's Wednesday. Cole wouldn't tell his mother anything, and this sounds more like a crime than an innocent prank."

Mrs. Levy was anxious to take the discovery to Cole for confirmation. "Mr. Wade, I need to go back home and talk to Cole. Can I call you later?"

"Certainly, Mrs. Levy. Please let me know how all this happened. We *will* find out who did this." As Ann left the office, Mr Jaymes turned toward the door ready to return to class. "No, Alan. You stay here. Tell me everything again from the beginning."

The second version was embellished and had a few omissions as well. The third story was even worse. After another half hour, Mr. Wade told Alan that he would get back to him when he heard back from Mrs. Levy.

Ann Levy arrived home to interrogate Cole. She hoped that revealing what she learned would prompt him to spill it all. Cole's anger grew as he first learned that his mom had gone to see Mr. Jaymes. He was ready to kill someone after she told him Alan's side of the story.

"There is only one truth in all of that. That man is weird and he kept staring at me instead of trying to help me."

"Oh, my God! Did he…"

"No, nothing like that. He showed up and eventually cut me loose after he got his eyes full." Cole then told her his facts of the past Sunday morning.

"Oh, Cole…I need to call Principal Wade."

"No."

"Well, that's not up for discussion. Before I call him, I need you to tell me everything that happened Saturday night. I need you to tell me how your privates ended up blue."

"He told you that?!" *I will kill him.*

23

Ann did not call for an appointment. Thursday morning, she was waiting on Principal Wade in the lobby. He told Barb to reschedule the meeting with the chair of the English Department and closed the door behind Mrs. Levy. "What else do you know?"

"First, two boys named Billy McCaster and Pete Dillard took Cole on something called a snipe hunt. The two boys quit and left Cole out there by himself holding the bag. At around 11:00 PM, Cole went looking for Billy and Pete and got a little turned around. He just wanted to walk home. He said that Billy and Pete snuck up on him from behind and that's the last thing he remembered before he woke up against that tree on Sunday morning. Now his story from this point differs greatly from Mr. Jaymes, and I am going to let you know upfront that I believe Cole." She laid out all the details of what happened from when Mr. Jaymes arrived until Cole asked him not to say anything about what had happened.

"Mrs. Levy, in light of this new information, I will question the boys and talk to Mr. Jaymes again. I will do this today, and I will call you back before Cole gets home."

"Cole is not coming to school. He said he can never come here again. He is embarrassed and afraid that the boys have bragged to everyone about what they did. Mostly, he can't face that Mr. Jaymes again, ever! He needs to be fired."

"Let me look into everything and I promise we will do the right thing here."

"I've never seen Cole like this before, Mr. Wade. I want to trust you, but this needs to be resolved soon. And this weekend, I am writing a letter to the school board about Mr. Jaymes's negligence."

As Ann left the office, Mr. Wade was already at work. "Barb, send for Billy McCaster and once he is in my office, send for Pete Dillard."

"Billy, come in and have a seat." Billy's armor was off. He was nervous and Mr. Wade could hear it in his voice and see it the way he carried his frame. "Do you know Cole Levy?"

"Yes, sir. We're friends and on the football team together." *And I love his sister.* "Is he OK? I haven't seen him or heard from him since Saturday night."

"Well, this meeting is about Saturday night. Mrs. Levy has come to see me and I need you to tell me everything that happened."

"Yes, sir. Pete helped me plan to get Cole out of the house for a while so I could be alone with my girlfriend, Emily. Emily is Cole's sister. Their mom was out of town for the weekend and we just wanted to be alone for a couple of hours. We decided to play a joke on Cole and take him snipe hunting. You know what that is, right?"

Mr. Wade nodded. *Of course, I do but I am not sure if Mrs. Levy or Cole do.*

"Pete and I left him around nine o'clock. Pete's mom picked him up at the school at 9:00 PM sharp. I went back over to Cole's house. I told Emily if he wasn't home by eleven, I would go get him. We lost track of time and soon after midnight, my mom busted in and made me go home. I wanted to see if Cole was in his room, but she made me just leave. I was restricted to my room on Sunday, with no phone or nothing. I saw Emily Monday morning and she said Cole was upset and not at school. I wanted to apologize, it was just a joke. We were becoming friends and it was just a little initiation or something."

"Tell me what you know about the paint. The blue paint."

"Huh. I don't know anything about any paint. Did the school get vandalized? I promise I didn't...."

Mr. Wade wanted to believe Billy but there were still many unanswered questions. "OK, Billy, I want you to wait outside of the office while I talk to Pete." He opened the door and signaled for Pete. Pete gave Billy a glance hoping to somehow garner a clue about what it was about. Billy's face gave lots of clues but Pete was forever a dim-bulb lapdog.

"Sit down, Pete." The door shut and the interrogation began.

Pete's story was different from Billy's. The most glaring difference was that he returned home at 11:00 PM, arriving via a drop-off by a couple of scrubs that he refused to name. After fifteen minutes, Mr. Wade recalled Billy to the office, "Barb, tell Billy to come back in." Billy entered and had a seat beside Pete. There was a nod but each knew it was not time to talk yet.

"Billy, your story matches Pete's story until nine. Pete said he got home at eleven and he was dropped off by two other boys. Billy, tell me who else was involved or you could both be facing expulsion."

"Pete, I saw you get in your mom's car just before nine and leave. I was pulling out of the lot. What..."

Pete interrupted, "Oh, yeah. Hang on. Mr. Wade, Billy didn't see me get in the car with the other boys. He just thought it was my mom."

Mr. Wade needed time to think. "OK, I need some time to sort this out. I am going to call your parents. 'Barb, ask Coach Selby to come to the office!' I'll..."

"No. No. Please don't tell Coach Selby." Both boys failed to realize that Coach Selby would have been the better alternative to their mothers.

Mr. Wade told them to be quiet. After letting them sweat for a few minutes, Coach Selby appeared. "Coach, escort these boys to ISS until I call for them."

Coach gave them a stinky eye.

"We didn't do anything bad, coach. I promise."

Coach Selby's face asked the question. Mr. Wade's shoulder shrug left hope that the boys might be right. Pete would pay a heavier price for protecting the scrubs. One week ISS from the principal, and a two-game suspension from Coach Selby. In Pete's orbit, naming the other boys had no upside. Besides, they didn't have anything to do with the prank. Pete knew they were bullies, so he decided to keep their names to himself.

24

Mr. Wade opened his office door and welcomed Mrs. McCaster and Mrs. Dillard. "Thank you for both coming in today. I do think it is important that we talk before the weekend. Last Saturday night the boys got caught up in something and I just need to communicate what has been said. Did the boys tell you anything?"

Laura's posture signaled Cookie to begin. "Yes, Billy and I have no secrets. I will tell you right now that I have a problem with you putting our boys in ISS for allegedly doing something on a weekend."

"Well, Mrs. McCaster, I agree except this happened on school property."

"Huh? I'm lost then. Are we talking about Saturday night? Billy was at Cole's house with his sister. I know this is true because I went to pick him up. Before that, he was with Pete all night. Billy brought Pete home around 11:00 PM and then went over to see Emily and Cole. I picked him up around 12:30 AM."

"That's right," Laura chimed in.

"Well, I can tell you that Billy was not with Pete after 9:00 PM. Pete was picked up at school by some other boys, and they took him home around eleven. Pete will not tell me their names. Billy was at Cole Levy's house with his sister, Emily, off and on from around 7:00 PM."

Mr. Wade then explained the plan, the snipe hunt, and finally, a carefully limited version of what happened to Cole Levy–a version that omitted Mr. Jaymes' involvement and Cole's nakedness. Dazed and confused, the mothers acknowledged the holes in their sons' stories.

25

Thursday afternoon, Ann received a call from the Principal at Foster Creek High School. After the conversation, Ann was convinced that neither boy had anything to do with what happened to Cole. She turned her attention to Emily.

"Is it true that you were with Billy McCaster on Saturday night, and you ignored my instructions to watch after your brother?"

Knowing she was caught, Emily had no choice but to surrender the truth.

"I love him and he loves me." It was clear that the whole truth would drip out slowly like a leaky faucet.

"That's ridiculous! You can't possibly be in love this fast."

Ann knew Emily would spill it all to her eventually but she had Cole to consider too. She also knew that the situation was dicey because Billy's father was the base commander and her husband's superior, and Mike's rank still didn't put them in the McCasters' inner circle. She long sensed that Cookie McCaster had measured her on their first encounter at the welcome luncheon. Her mind was racing, and she made the quick and final decision to just bury what happened and remove Cole from any situation that might remind him of the events of Saturday night. In Ann's mind, it would be too embarrassing to *her*. She wanted to retire and steady herself with a few drinks. By the time the arguing with Emily ended around 10:00 PM, Ann Levy grabbed a bottle and escaped to a different reality. A reality where she was a victim, not Cole. A reality where alcohol was her only comfort.

Ann slept late Friday morning, She didn't bother checking on Cole. She knew he would not return to FCHS. She remembered her hastily made plans from the night before and picked up the phone book. She looked up the number for a private boarding school that she remembered from her trip to Charleston. She remembered Froggy talking about it at the bar. Perhaps Froggy had children that he sent there, but she only vaguely remembered the details.

Bishop Porter Academy, 1814 River Road, Charleston, 884-2436.

She dialed the number and asked for admissions. "My name is Ann Levy. I have a son, Cole, who is a sophomore and I was hoping that you might have an immediate opening for him. We recently moved from Indiana, and he is having a difficult time adjusting to the public school here."

"Mom. What are you doing?" Cole had heard just enough to know that something was amiss.

Ann covered the phone and shushed him. "Yes. We can be there for a tour at 1:30. Do you have sports? Cole is a great football player."

"Mom, please."

"Perfect. Can we meet the coach while we are there?" She paused and Cole's interest had changed a little.

Cole thought that perhaps a change would help him not have to deal with Billy and Pete ever again. It would also mean he would never have to face Mr. Jaymes again. And finally, he realized he could leave his mother to her bottle and not have to pretend that he did not know of her transgressions.

Ann hung up the phone and readied herself for an argument.

"Now Cole, your father..."

Cole cut her off. He was tired of all of it. It was fight or flight and Cole was ready to fly.

"Mom, just don't bother. I want to go see the place. Where is it? Far away I hope."

"It is on the Ashley River in Charleston. Over near The Citadel, I think."

"How far away is that?"

"About 30 minutes."

Cole was hoping for time in hours not minutes. "Okay. I am going to shower. I'll be ready to leave at 12:30."

Ann did not risk further discussion. She would let him know of the boarding later on. As she turned to have a morning quickie with Jack Daniels, she mustered up enough strength to let him down easy this time.

After a quick swig straight from the bottle, she looked lovingly toward the label, "I will have to see you later tonight, love."

It was a date she would not keep.

26

At 12:30 PM sharp, Cole emerged from his room and headed directly to the minivan. Ann grabbed the keys and her purse and followed him out the door. Janet was crossing the front lawn as they were nearing the minivan. Janet had become her favorite and most reliable drinking buddy, but they had not spoken since they returned from their weekend getaway to Charleston. Janet greeted Ann and asked, "Can we talk? Maybe you can come by when you get back."

"Maybe."

The neighbor recognized something was amiss. Ann seemed more out of control than normal and Cole's eyes were heavy and looked burdened. As the Levys got in and backed away, Janet thought, *She must already know.*

"Buckle up, Cole." Ann's voice was deliberate. Her mind was racing and conflicted. She kept reassessing the conflicts in her mind, and she concluded she was doing the right thing. She could sense Cole was different than this morning. She couldn't decide if his current state was relief or anger. She had never seen him like this. She decided not to speak until they had completed the visit. Unless Cole wanted to talk, she would not.

The ride to the west of the Ashley River was silent and took forty-five minutes. Both Cole and Ann internally reflected upon the recent events. There was no eye contact, both being content in their thoughts. Ann pulled into the long winding drive leading up to the school. It was lined with live oaks with undergrowth of azaleas. It reminded her of

Cookie McCaster's manicured gardens and lawn at the Naval Weapons Station. They pulled into a one-way arched parking area in front of a white stone building. Ann noticed a sign directing visitors to the dorms and cafeteria. She hoped Cole did not notice it. She glanced in his direction and noted that he missed the dorm sign, as he was looking over at a sign directing students and visitors to the gym and stadium. Cole cataloged a check.

"Admissions this way," Ann interrupted his thoughts.

"Admissions? Aren't you putting the cart before the horse?"

"It is just where we go for the tour."

Cole had no further response. Ann opened the door, and Cole was met by a uniformed guy about his age.

"Hello and welcome to BPA. My name is Chad Russell. Are you Cole?"

"Yes."

"Well, it's great to meet you, Cole." Chad extended his hand which concluded with a firm handshake. Cole was used to this, as everyone associated with the military learned early on how to do a proper handshake. 'Web to web then close firmly and shake' his dad had drilled him until he mastered it. Cole knew when a handshake was sincere or tentative. He could tell that Chad was both sincere and confident. Chad withdrew his hand and turned toward Ann.

"You must be Mrs. Levy," as he extended his hand. Chad could also read a handshake, and he could tell Ann Levy lacked confidence. "I was asked to meet you and accompany you on your tour if that is OK with you, Cole."

Cole already felt more welcomed here than at any time at Foster Creek High School. "Sure, that'd be great," he responded and then added, "It would be nice to get a perspective from someone my age."

"Oh yeah! I think it helps to get to know the school from another student. I loved my tour weekend when I came to visit BPA. I am still good friends with Andy, the student who was my guide for that weekend. Andy and I both play football and basketball here. Do you like sports, Cole?"

"I play football. Receiver. More specifically slot. We were just starting spring practice at my other school. Are you in spring practice?"

"No. Coach Stoltz is the head coach of our baseball team as well, and we start spring practice after baseball season ends. Coach Stoltz is also our head football coach. We will stop by the baseball field later, and I will introduce you before they start practice. He wants to meet everyone, even if they might be unsure if they want to play here."

"That would be great," Ann added but was met with a menacing glance from Cole that signaled her to butt out.

As they finished the small talk, they arrived at a large wood-paneled door with a small plaque that read 'Admissions.' As Chad opened the door, Ann was greeted by a polite and personable gentleman whose name tag read 'Mr. James Monroe, *Director of Admissions.*'

"Welcome to Bishop Porter Academy, Mrs. Levy." Again with the handshakes and then a redirect to Cole. "Cole, I see you have met Chad. He is going to accompany us and answer any questions that y'all might have."

"Yes, that would be great." Ann did not look toward Cole this time.

27

The tour began in the administration building and the group quickly moved out the back door of the building just as a bell rang. The door opened onto a large lawn that quickly filled with students scurrying from one building to another.

"The buildings straight ahead are our academic halls. The left building is mostly science and math but we do use some classrooms in the building when we need an extra section of humanities. The hall beside it is the humanities building. You know, English, social studies, foreign languages. Most kids here take Latin. As you can see from our cadets, we are a military prep school, but you are not required to enter a service upon graduation. We have students that are accepted at prestigious universities all across the country."

Cole noticed most students were moving between these two buildings. He glanced in the direction of a two-story brick building to the left. "Is that the gym?"

Chad chimed in, "That is the ROTC building. And these buildings to the right are our dorms and cafeteria."

"Dorms?" Cole tried to cover up his surprise. "So why are some guys going to the dorm now?"

"Great question, Cole. Students have a study hall as one of their periods every day. Girls and boys that participate in athletics have the last period as a study hall and in their season, they go to practice. We are lucky in football because we always use the period to lift or practice."

"So how many classes do you take?"

"Most take five, but some pass on study hall and take six."

"So the building between the two dormitories is..."

"The cafeteria." Mr. Monroe interjected. "We serve three meals a day and a morning and afternoon snack cart in the school. Meals and snacks are all included in the cost of attendance. But we will go over all that later."

"The food is delicious," Chad was quick to add.

They made their way forward reaching the doors of the halls where classes were conducted. Several cute girls smiled and seemed to flirt with Cole. Chad would nod at him and wink. Once inside they peeked in a class or two and noticed that although the arrangements seemed the same as any other school, the culture was different. The teachers had the respect of the students, and the students seemed to be engaged. Cole put another check on the "pro" side of his mental ledger.

The group then walked along a stark white sidewalk that led to the boys' dorm. Chad and Cole passed on talking about classes and instead focused on the girls. Cole wondered what it would be like to live so close to a bunch of girls with no parents anywhere. As they reached the dorm, the door flew open, "I am Ms. Fields, and I am the house mother."

That explains that. Cole sized up Ms. Fields instantly and he could tell by her demeanor that she was not to be tested. Chad's facial expressions confirmed it.

"Well, first I will say that girls are not to visit the boys' dorm and vice versa. Our first floor has two-person suites for upperclassmen. Our second floor has three-person suites for underclassmen. Since you will be a junior next year, you would have one roommate and live on the first floor. Chad is on the second floor with two cadets in a suite, one of whom hosted him when he came last year. Since it is late in the year, if you came this year, Chad would be your roommate, and you would both move on down to the first floor. Do you know if you will be attending for the summer yet?"

Ann felt things moving a little fast, but before she could answer, Cole said, "We haven't decided yet." Ann was now struggling with the notion that Cole would even consider being away from her.

After touring the suite, Cole surmised that the room was much larger than any room ever assigned by Navy housing. The sleeping area had two bunks that were lofted with a desk area underneath each. The bunks were aligned in an L-shape and each cadet had a larger chest with drawers on one side and a hangup area on the other. There was a half-wall that partitioned the sleeping area and on the other side was a small area with a sofa, chair, table, and lamps. "You may put up posters if you like, but you are responsible for any damage. If you have a TV, it can go on the table beside the bathroom door." Cole thought almost out loud 'Wow, a bathroom where I *on't have to share with Emily.' Cole put another check on the good side of the ledger.

"Cole, I want to get you over to Coach before he starts practice. Do you have any questions so far?" Mr. Monroe said.

"Everything is good so far," Cole said this in a way to both make Ann feel guilty that he would so easily choose this life over the one that she provided, and to express a growing excitement over the opportunity.

Boys started gathering as they made their way to the baseball field. The field was adjacent to the football stadium, a small 'stadium' with maybe four rows for spectators that lined the complete length of the field on both sides. As they edged closer to the baseball field, Cole noticed only metal bleachers, but an exceptionally maintained field. He could see an oddly- shaped man in the distance who was beginning to gather everyone for what looked like a warm-up run. The pack of about fifteen boys departed as they jogged around 3rd base on their way to the outfield. The coach turned toward them just as they approached. Ann gasped. It was Froggy.

28

A thousand thoughts ran through his mind as Gerald Stoltz turned and saw Ann directly in front of him. *Was she here to rat me out for some breach of ethics or the code of conduct I signed with the school?* He remembered every detail of the night they spent together. He had failed to realize how drunk Ann was at the time, but he recalled how into it she was, how she needed more every time he wanted to just go to sleep. Finally, he remembered how distant she became the next morning. *Maybe she hunted me down. Oh my God, she can't already be pregnant. No, that can't...*

Before he could think of anything else, he gathered himself and realized that there was a young man with her, an athletic looking one, to boot. He heard the sounds of the introductions, but wasn't actively listening.

"I am Cole Levy. It is nice to meet you, Coach," as Cole extended his hand.

"I am Coach Stoltz, the head baseball and football coach here." His eyes darted back and forth between Ann and Cole. *Ok, she is here with her son for a tour. She looks very uncomfortable.* "It is very nice to meet you both." He gave Ann a reassuring nod.

"Yes, very nice to meet you, sir." Ann was relieved that at least for now, Froggy seemed to be willing to keep their secret. *He seems to be nicer than I remember. He cleaned up well. Not as short as I thought. Hmm...I wonder. Stop Ann. Stop it right now. You are the worst mother ever.*

The pack was almost finished with their lap, and Cole noticed a group of boys that were all in good shape. He quickly measured himself up to them and accepted that he could compete with these athletes if they played football, too. Coach Stoltz gathered them as they came around home plate. "Boys, this is Cole Levy."

The team was panting slightly but each one took time to shake Cole's hand and welcome him. Ann sensed a happiness in Cole she had not seen since San Diego.

Andy Orr was a tall, lanky player that was the first to speak after the handshakes. "Chad and I are roommates. I was his host when he toured here with his family. We have to get started with practice here soon, but I hope to get to know you better this weekend. You are staying for the weekend visit, right?"

Chad chimed in, "Yes, we hope you will stay for an extended visit. We have the visitor's suite for the weekend. There is a home doubleheader tomorrow, and we have drills in the morning. It sounds bad, but it is honestly a little fun." Cole could hear a few boys grunt from the back, but most were nodding.

Coach said, This group, of course, gets a pass tomorrow because of the game. It is actually a great weekend as most students are staying here this weekend. This is the last home game of the year and after an away game Tuesday, they get a week off before we start spring football practice for three weeks."

It sounded great to Cole. He could get far away from his rivals at the base and not risk seeing anyone. He was also tired of being cooped up.

"Mom?"

Ann pursed her lips and rocked her head slightly side to side as if she was considering it. "We didn't know about this and he came unprepared. I don't..."

Chad's eyes lit up as he interrupted, "We have guest uniforms for all overnight and weekend visitors. We have a commissary and he can pick up a toothbrush and any other items he may need for a weekend there. Really, this is something that we are used to."

Mr. Monroe was standing to the side and nodding with approval at how well Chad was conducting himself. "Chad is correct. We will take good care of Cole. It would be great if he could sit in on some classes Monday, as well. So if you could wait and pick him up after lunch on Monday, we can talk more about admissions and cost then. We have all sorts of financial aid here and 75% of our cadets receive some amount which varies from 25% to a full scholarship. Students with full rides usually play a sport. It is up to the coach to decide how much to disperse to the athlete. Do you play a sport, Cole?"

"Yes, I play football."

Coach Stoltz cracked an even wider smile and thought out loud "Receiver?"

"Yes sir."

Ann interrupted, "Is this something you want to do Cole?"

"Absolutely," he said without hesitation.

Final arrangements were made and Ann prepared to leave. She said her goodbyes and as she drove away, she peered through the rain on the window and realized Cole's indifference toward her. When she got to the end of the tree-lined drive, tears began to flow as everything began to take a toll. She tried to gather herself. She tried to reassure herself by speaking aloud, "Well, I will see him on Monday. Everything will be OK. I can focus on Emily now. Oh, shit!"

At that point, she remembered the way she left things with Emily, and the tears flowed more freely.

29

As if Ann wasn't tormented enough, the late afternoon Friday traffic on the interstate was accompanied by a classic low country late afternoon thunderstorm. Charleston was hot in the late spring and summer and the humidity made the car windows fog on the inside. Ann deemed it too hot to turn on the defroster. Even with conditions worsening and demanding more of her attention, Ann still couldn't escape her thoughts. She tried desperately to remember the details of the night that she spent with Coach Stoltz. Froggy was in the past. Now, he had a name and her thoughts about him were shiny and new as she polished up the tarnished memories of the man she met at the bar. She revisited why she would do such a thing. She told herself how lucky she was to have secured Mike Levy, only to remind herself that she resented the life he had given her.

Mike cares only about work and the kids. And his concern for his children is slightly questionable since he stashes all that money and doesn't provide for his family the way he should. He never does anything for me. And I hate that stupid boat in Crane. Why do I always have to be the one to deal with the bullshit? Mike is such a coward. But he has no problem trying to control me.

She was spiraling down. She wrestled in her mind, and the exercise was making her winded. She was having a difficult time catching her breath. She could feel the knots in her stomach, the pain from her neck radiating to her shoulders, and her tightening chest. She never recognized an oncoming panic attack, but she knew exactly how to manage one. This particular wrestling would end or be the end of her.

I will be home soon, and I can settle myself down. I just need a drink and a good night's sleep. And I hate the way Mike belittles me about having a drink.

She was rambling on as the miles passed.

It's not like I have a real problem. Coach Stoltz didn't seem to care that I was drinking at that bar. He was there drinking, too. And Mike picked me up at a bar. Hypocrite! I just need to forget about that night in Charleston. Coach has too much to lose to tell anyone, so I will just bury this along with everything else.

The knots grew larger. Finally, she was on Sunset Drive. It was still pouring, but her thoughts had kept her so occupied that she barely noticed. The rain was ponding over the neighborhood streets. As she pulled into the driveway, she was shocked to see Janet dart from her adjacent home under cover from her umbrella. She glanced in that direction.

She must really need to have a drink to be out in this shit. Huh, not as much as me.

"Ann, are you OK? I am so sorry. I wanted to tell you before. Who told you?" Janet had already concluded that Ann's state confirmed she was too late.

Ann looked puzzled. "Told me what? Nobody told me anything. Has something else happened?" *Please don't tell me you know about what happened to Cole. Please no. I don't know what he will do. No, what I will do.*

"Oh Ann, I have terrible news. Can you come over?"

The door opened and Emily appeared. "MOM!"

Janet now concluded Ann had not heard, but that Emily already knew their secret. She grabbed Ann's arm and quickly turned her toward her, "The whole neighborhood is gossiping about what happened to you in Charleston last weekend. Ann, I didn't tell anybody anything. Lori blabbed to everyone about you and that man and now it's all over the base."

Ann's jaw dropped as the rain mixed with a fresh stream of tears. She could hear Emily continue to scream for her. She told Janet that she was likely her only friend, and she desperately needed a drink but didn't have any stamina left to deal with this now. She was drenched as she walked toward the front door.

30

As Ann hurried toward the door, she could see that the puddles in Emily's eyes were not from the rain. "I am so sorry. I can fix this."

Emily's face tightened from the shock that her mother already knew *her* secret. "How did you know? I haven't told anyone, not even Billy."

At that very moment Ann felt relief. *Why would she tell Billy first anyway. This can't be about me. At least not yet.* She felt her anxiety shutting her down and she was choking on her words, "Are we talking about the same thing here?"

Emily heard the shakiness in her mom's voice and realized it, too. She sensed her mom didn't really have her faculties about her. It was not like most days when she was simply hungover, on the verge of being drunk or totally wasted. There was rarely a day without drama and she would be determined that today's drama would be headlined by her.

"Can you please not make this about you, Mom? I need you to not have a pity party here when I tell you this."

Ann was exasperated. She clammed up. Her tank was empty, and she had not an ounce of fortitude remaining. Utter silence was her response. She stared blankly at Emily,

"Well, Mom. You can't actually fix this." Emily did have the fortitude that her mom lacked. She almost felt empathy for her. She had not even given a thought about Cole's whereabouts. *No, don't give in to her games.*

"I am pregnant. I haven't told Billy yet, so if you could please…"

Ann's mouth gaped open but only the wind escaped as she bent over to her knees. In an instant, she was upright, tightly pulling her bag into her breasts. She opened her eyes and turned to grab the keys she had just minutes ago set in the plastic tupperware bowl on the table beside their front door. She hastily returned to the rush of rain hoping it would wash away her pain. She opened the door to the van and as she closed the door, she wiped a small patch of condensation from the glass in front of her so she could see. She saw Emily waving frantically and opened the door only to hear her daughter say, "That's right, Mom. Run away somewhere. Don't worry about..."

That was the last of what she heard as she slammed the door shut. She could see Emily talking to air as she backed out of the drive. The storm was more turbulent now, but nothing rivaled the turbulence within her. As she drove away, she realized that Emily would never see her in the same way again. It was the coup de grâce.

Ann turned left off Sunset Drive onto the main road that led to the Weapons Station. She could barely focus through the unyielding rain. As she looked to both sides of the road, she could see the swell of the creek flooding over the marshy land onto the road. The pine needles were blowing across the windshield reminding her that she was nearing the forested area close to the gate. Doubts began to surface.

I don't want to talk to that bitch, Cookie. This is too much.

B-dum, B-dum, B-dum. She could hear her heart pounding harder with each beat. She spotted the tall pine trees playing hide and seek in the dense rain and impulsively altered her plan.

B-dum, B-dum.

She accelerated and veered right, sending a spray of water from the creek high into the air. "That's the one."

She had no regrets. Her van kissed the intended target, then the mangled mess, now splattered with a bright red hue, bounced its way back into the muddy gray water.

B-dum, B-dum, B----

31

Whack. The MPs in the pillbox heard the crash and looked down the road just in time to see a larger spray of water as the car entered the swollen banks of the creek. They could see the tangled metal and both realized that nobody could have survived that. The guards jumped into action, calling the station police as they efficiently covered the 150 yards to the scene only to find a redheaded woman void of life, still managing a faint smile.

More military personnel arrived, including a medic who confirmed the MPs assessment of her condition. The Mortuary Affairs Specialist was called and arrived with transport within fifteen minutes. The MPs carefully opened the crumpled door panel, and the body was removed, and then tagged according to protocol. MPs worked in unison to ID her, finding her wallet in a large purse. They found a license issued from Indiana with the name Ann B. Levy. They also found a military-issued commissary badge that confirmed the identity.

"Someone needs to escalate this up the chain of command."

A call was made from the jeep and the appropriate officers were notified. The MPs placed the body into a large black plastic-zippered bag. It was then loaded onto the military ambulance and sent down the road toward the base. The rain had stopped, but the sky still looked threatening. The scene moved quickly from rescue, to recovery, to investigation. Heavy rains had prevented any skid marks on the road. Perhaps if there were any, the investigators could confirm if there was an effort to correct the course from a sudden swerve from a blowout or mechanical failure. Perhaps. An investigation would conclude with no clear evidence as to the cause. It would be logged as an accident. There would be no evidence that would ever point to any other conclusion, at least to everyone that was objective.

Eventually, the news arrived in the office of Commander McCaster. Andrew McCaster was a cool, collected, and respected leader who did not overreact and seemed to always make the right call. He asked the reporting officer if they had the name of the husband. The reporting officer knew he better have it.

"Yes sir. His name is CWO Mike Levy, and he is currently cruising on the USS Sturgeon, sir."

"Let's radio Chief Fiora and tell him what has happened," The commander started, as if dictating. The officer pulled a small pad and pen from his pockets and began taking notes.

"Levy seems to be a few days out before they are going to make port, and we can't send another ship to those waters anyway. You know how the North Sea is this time of year. They have kids, right?"

"Yes sir, two children, a daughter Emily, age 17. She will be 18 in a few weeks, and a son, Cole, age 16."

"I need a firm timeline on Levy and when we can get him here. Get Ritter to help you with that. Tell the chaplain to be ready in 15 minutes. We need to go to the house and tell these kids. Civilians probably saw the vehicle, and we need to get to the kids before someone else does. They're on their own for at least a few days and both are minors. We don't want any loose threads here. Until we get word back from CWO Levy, we need to have a plan. You and Ritter will need to bring anyone else that you involve up to speed on any plans, firm or potential. I want to be briefed on our way to see those kids so I have some options. Start with a list of relatives. Better get to it."

"Yes sir." The officer turned and left as the commander was already phoning home.

Cookie picked up the phone on the second ring. "Hello."

Andrew explained he would be late for dinner. Navy wives knew their husbands would never give details. "I will put a plate in the oven for you. Roast Beef. Your favorite."

"That would be great. Bye, honey." It was their code. She knew the added endearment meant it was important but not to national security. There was never a code for that.

32

It had been three hours since her mom left. That was enough time for Emily to have a cage match with her emotions. Currently, *guilt* was entering the ring. She desperately needed to apologize to her mom for the cruelty of her words. She meant them, but Mike Levy had taught her long ago not to shoot all your bullets until you must.

And where is Cole? He hasn't left the house in a week. Did Mom take him somewhere? She never tells me shit.

As she finished that thought, she saw a parade of official Navy vehicles turn onto her street. She recognized the insignia on the front car and knew it was the chaplain. It almost always meant that a serviceman's life was lost.

Well, that family is going to have a worse night than us.

As she summed up her thoughts, the caravan slowed and came to a stop in front of the house. The chaplain inhaled and his shoulders clenched and then dropped on a long exhale as he opened the door. Emily sobbed as her shaky voice met the party. "Is it my Dad?"

She almost didn't recognize Billy's father until he said, "Is your brother home? Can we come in, Emily?"

They know my name. They know Cole's name. Where is Cole? They didn't ask to see Mom. Oh no! "It's Mom. Oh my God!" She stared straight through the chaplain as she received the confirmation. She would wear the weight of her guilt for years to come.

The neighbors were gawking from their respective driveways. Janet could see Emily's distress and came and wrapped her arm around her as they entered the home.

"I am so sorry for the mess," Emily said, shaking. Voice quivering, Emily said, "You asked if Cole was home. I have not seen him all day. He didn't go to school this week, and he was not here when Mom came home. Please tell me what happened."

The words were forced, and there were short breaths in mid-sentence. She listened carefully as they told her of the accident. They tried to comfort her by telling her it was quick and that her mother likely died on impact and didn't suffer. Emily knew her mother had suffered for years, and she, once again, thought of the tumultuous last moments with her mom. Her eyes were completely full, and she was comforted by the embrace of her neighbor. Her mom's only friend, and now the likely only connection to her until she could see her father and Cole.

"We need to find your brother. Any idea where he might be? He doesn't need to hear about this elsewhere."

Janet put on *that* hat again. She already planned to clean the house. She then suggested to the Commander that she stay with Emily and wait for Cole. "He left with Ann after lunch but he wasn't with her when she came back."

Before the agreed-upon plan could be conveyed, Billy's dad spoke. "We will have the chaplain stay with you for a while, as well."

The officers rarely saw Andrew McCaster veer from a plan once his mind was made up. They glanced at each other and gave an understanding nod.

"We have been in contact with your dad's boat, and we will get him on a plane on Monday morning. With the time difference, we should have him here at 0940."

Emily eventually gently squirmed away from Janet's clutch. It had been comforting, but it had been an hour since the officers left, and she couldn't handle too much more of the chaplain's attempt at reconciling what happened. After waiting twenty more minutes for Cole, she departed for her room.

"When Cole gets here, please let me know."

"Of course, dear." Janet turned back toward the chaplain. After moments of awkward silence, Janet stood as she softly spoke, "Those poor children. I am going to clean up the kitchen and run the vacuum. You know, just tidy things up a bit."

The chaplain stood and without speaking began organizing some of the clutter in the room. As he finished, Janet turned off the faucet and loud sounds of clinking dishes distracted him. He noticed an old *Filter Queen* canister vacuum neatly stowed in a cubby underneath the shelves of food in the kitchen. He plugged it in, flipped the silver switch and got lost in the exaggerated shrill sounds whirling from the unit. Emily briefly appeared to check on the noise before quickly retreating to her room after noting Cole was still unaccounted for.

33

Andrew McCaster had a long day. After a couple more hours with staff, he had a driver take him home. The house looked peaceful on the outside. He thought of Cookie and upon seeing the azaleas at their peak that morning, of how appreciative he was that Cookie had them maintained so meticulously each year, just for these few weeks of awe-inspiring beauty. He passed by the last shrub and noticed the creek, although still swollen, was subsiding. He entered the home to find Cookie waiting at the table holding an issue of *Southern Living* in her hands. She closed the magazine and said, "Dinner is in the oven. Come sit down, and I will get it for you. Do you want tea or something else?"

"Tea would be great. Probably something else after dinner. It has been a long day. I see Billy is still here on a Friday night. How much longer is he on house arrest?"

As she delivered the food, she turned and poured herself a cup of coffee. It was nearly 2230 when she sat down and steadied herself to listen. "Just a little while longer. We can talk about that more tomorrow." She had planned to talk about Billy tonight but that would have to wait now.

"Can you tell me what is going on?"

As he conveyed the events of the day to his wife, neither had noticed Billy standing nearby in the kitchen. Billy fought back tears, but his parents could see the glaze in his eyes as he said, "Dad, I know Emily Levy and I play football with Cole. Emily and I have been dating for a while now, but Mom is trying to break us up. I need to go to her now."

Billy looked at his mom and saw a face flush with shock. Although he did not require a response, he was demanding one and he was willing to put up a fight this time, even in front of his still stoic father.

"You are not going until the storm passes." Cookie's voice was trembling but she was adamant when she met Billy's demand.

Billy turned toward the window before the words escaped from Cookie's pursed lips. The drizzle quickly stopped, and the sky turned from gray to include patches of midnight blue.

"I see stars through the clouds now, Dad. And it's not raining anymore. Please."

Cookie knew this was Andrew's call. Even though it was very late, the commander gave his quick approval with a stipulation that he needed to be back by 2400. Billy wiggled the keys from his Levi's as the screen door creaked and then slammed against the iron frame.

Billy was at the stoop of the Levy house five minutes later. The chaplain knew Billy and concluded he would not be there without express permission from Commander McCaster.

"Hello, Billy. I am sorry, but Cole is not here."

"I'm here to see Emily."

Emily appeared from her room as Billy entered the house. She ran and fell into his arms.

"Oh, Billy," her voice choking back her emotions. "Something terrible has happened." She wanted to say more but the words would not come out.

"I am so sorry, Emily. My dad told me. What can I do?"

"Just this," as Emily reacted to his comforting embrace.

34

Cole and Chad entered the barracks on the first floor. Soon after, Ms. Fields arrived with a small duffle.

"I hear that you are with us until Monday. I have all four uniforms you will need and some shoes. Chad will fill you in on when to wear what." She was military all the way. "Dinner is always at 1800, so better hustle."

"That means 6 PM," Chad volunteered as Ms. Fields quickly scurried away.

"Yeah, we're a Navy family, so I know the drill. We always eat at 1800, and my dad insists on punctuality. My sister, Emily, is usually the only one that tests him."

"Well, you'll fit in well here." As they unpacked the clothes, Chad added, "Basically, just pick out the same uniform that I wear every day. This is for school and dinner. The dress blues are for church Sunday, and the khakis and light blue shirt are for drills tomorrow. There is a name tag to pin on each until you get a stitched tag."

The boys took note that the tags had been inked with "LEVY." Cole stripped out of his civilian clothes and slipped on his gray woolen trousers. The trousers had navy blue piping on the outer seams that gave the slacks a trim, tailored look. He mirrored Chad completely and the confidence he gained from the uniform was confirmed when Chad heard less rasp in Cole's voice as he said, "Let's eat."

"Let's do it. By the way, my parents sometimes come by on Friday to eat with me when I stay for the weekend. You will like them if you get to meet them."

"Do you get along with them? My dad works all the time and my mom, well that's a whole other story," as the rasp began to return.

"Yeah, they are *great*! You'll see. Maybe you can even come home with me for a weekend. We live further out on James Island close to Folly Beach. Have you been to the beach?"

"Not here. But when I was younger, in San Diego. We moved to Indiana when I was six, I think. We just moved here in January." Cole realized he was saying too much and was happy that they arrived at the mess hall. "We're here."

"And my parents are here too," Chad waved back, advancing toward them, prodding Cole with a hand on his shoulder.

"Mom, Dad, this is Cole Levy. He is visiting this weekend, and I am his host."

Mr. and Mrs. Russell enthusiastically greeted Cole. "It is a pleasure meeting you, Cole. Are you visiting or enrolling here? This is an amazing school and Chad loves it. We are so proud of him."

Chad was a little embarrassed and cut them off. "Mom, please." Everyone chuckled.

"Well, let's eat then. I hope they have meatloaf tonight. It's our favorite." Mr. Russell had gotten the hint.

"Well, it's *your* favorite Sam," Betty Russell quipped.

"It's really good, Cole. One of my favorites for sure."

"One of mine also." It was true but Cole was just trying to fit in.

The family was served a generous portion of meatloaf, green beans, mashed potatoes, a roll, and a slice of apple pie. Of course, a tall glass of sweet tea to drink was nothing like Cole had ever tasted. He thought it was like drinking syrup. After half a glass, he reached for the water pitcher at the table and opted to dilute the rest. *Perfect.* There was plenty of conversation around the table as the Russells seemed to be very familiar with the other two boys from Chad's suite.

Cole was attentive but he really perked up when he heard one of the boys say, "Well, your boat is fantastic. Deep sea fishing was the highlight of our summer. How many red snapper did we get? Over twenty?"

"Something like that. We will definitely do that again." Mr. Russell noticed the sparkle in Cole's eyes. "We would love to have you come too, Cole."

"For sure." *What was that?* 'I mean, yes sir." Chuckles again.

Mrs. Russell had a reassuring smile as she said, "Chad is already rubbing off on you."

After the last bites of the apple pie, the boys decided that it would be a card night. Spades would be the game and after the Russells left, the boys made their way back to the dorm. They changed into their shorts and tees, carefully hung up their clothes, and met back in the common area. Andy reminded them of the double-header tomorrow and that the game would need to end at 10:30 PM sharp. Tegan partnered with Chad leaving Andy with Cole. Cole was a skillful player having been mentored by his father. They used to play with another dad and his son on rec nights in Crane. It wasn't a close match. Even when Andy and Cole didn't have a great hand, they still managed to finesse poor Tegan out of an easy trick. Cole felt more accepted in two hours than in three months in Foster Creek. Cole realized his quiet demeanor was an asset here, not the liability it usually was in trying to make friends. Chad and Andy were outwardly personable enough. The boys appreciated how Cole didn't boast about the cards, and he was quickly making new friends. Three was always an awkward number for them anyway and two alphas in a room was one too many. Tegan's quiet nature offset Andy's big personality.

At 2300, Cole fell fast asleep, and for the first night since Mr. Jaymes found him, his dreams were not of blue paint, but that of an azure sky reflecting on a deep blue sea. In his dream, he and his new friends were standing and smiling on a *Boston Whaler*, holding a rod, and reeling in a bounty of red snapper.

35

Gerald Stoltz did not sleep well that night. He thought of every possible thing that could go wrong. It was this very kind of thinking that led to an end to his marriage. He couldn't afford to lose his job, as it meant his twin daughters, rising seniors, could lose their scholarships. Although they didn't live with him, he could see them every day. The girls were typical teens and tried to avoid him whenever they could.

He decided the best way to protect his interests was to advocate for Cole. He knew the academy would likely offer an active military award of 50%. Mr. Monroe saw the NAVY emblem on the van as Ann had left, and passed the info onto Coach. The athletic scholarship he would recommend would cover the rest. After little rest, Gerald arose, showered, dressed, and was out the door,

He arrived promptly at 0730 hoping to meet Cole as they left breakfast. The school operated in a machine-like manner, and as the bell tower belted a single chime on the half-hour, Coach Stoltz greeted the boys.

"Cole, can I speak to you for a moment? I won't be long, Chad. I know you have to get ready for drill practice."

"Yes sir," as Cole looked him squarely in the eye.

"Well, I would like to see if you could help our football team next year. I have a good eye for picking athletes. I don't know your financial situation, but it could mean some scholarship money for you. Can you carve out some time this afternoon?"

Cole had begun to think about the cost, too. He was relieved to hear first that the coach thought of him as an athlete, and secondly that a scholarship could be had. The campus awoke all his senses. He had slept well and didn't have to wake up to the smell of his mother. Breakfast was substantial, and he was full of energy.

"What do you want me to do?" His gravelly voice seemed more confident now.

"Well, after the baseball games, I will have Chad and Alec, our QB, meet us at the football field, and I would like you to run some routes if you are up to it." The coach set his plan in motion.

"Yes sir, but I only have the sneakers that I came with."

"No worries, we always have some extra cleats. I can issue them to you, and you can use them for spring practice and next year if they still fit. Better get going to drills, son."

"Yes sir." Cole jogged toward the door to find Chad waiting. He gave Chad his instructions and asked about Alec.

"Awesome. Alec is a great QB. He plays baseball, too, so I will point him out when we go to the game."

Chad's eyes grew wider. "That's not going to pass inspection. Look at mine. See how the sheet is taut under the blanket?"

Cole stripped the cover and top sheet off his bunk and started over. Chad pointed out some of the finer details about making up a bed, and Cole was required to redo it twice more. They moved on to other Saturday morning duties like polishing Chad's brass. They moved to the shoes, and Cole wondered why they needed to polish them before drills if they were just going to get dirty. They changed into their PT uniforms and were out the door.

"What should I expect?" Cole was asking about the tryout, but Chad began explaining drill and PT.

"We don't practice for the parade on Saturdays since so many cadets go home on the weekend. Today we will just do physical training and marching. Lots of push-ups, sit-ups, and marching. Then more calisthenics and more marching. We must march in unison and at a constant pace. Usually an hour on Saturday. It all starts at 0900."

Cole glanced at the clock. "What do we do now?"

Just as he heard another chime, there was a bang on the door. Ms. Fields was standing behind two senior cadets. "Inspection!"

Chad stood at attention as they entered the room. Cole tried to mimic Chad's posture, and the cadets seemed to appreciate the effort.

"Very good cadet." The last boy exited in formation and as the door closed, the boys got an approving nod from Ms. Fields as they heard a bang on the next door, "Inspection!"

"How often does this happen?"

"For underclassmen, every day but Sunday. But it is expected to be regulation on Sunday too. Many cadets never leave campus and if they have visitors, it is always on Sunday. We have a kid in our hall from Chicago, and he never goes anywhere. For upperclassmen, inspection is on Monday, Wednesday, Friday, and Saturday. Almost everyone is back on campus in time for Sunday dinner, because it's always fried chicken."

"I see. Like KFC?"

"Not even close."

Cole got a glimpse of himself in the mirror. "Is the emblem on my T-shirt the school crest or something?"

"Yep, same as the gold one on the bottom of the navy shorts. The school calls it an insignia."

"I see." Cole felt athletic in his uniform and as the boys approached the quad, Cole was surprised to find that all of the cadets looked to be in good shape. He didn't see any that looked like Pete, and they all looked more athletic than him.

As inspection was completed, the rest of the boys spilled out of the barracks and walked in formation to the manicured lawn. At 0900, the ninth chime sounded and the activity began.

"Jumping Jacks. Ready, exercise. One and two and three and…" blasted from a megaphone held by a military man standing on a stoop.

Cole was steady, but he felt slightly intimidated as he just focused on keeping time with the jumping jacks. He felt rewarded as he completed more exercises in unison with the other cadets. They marched, and he kept a perfect pace. His confidence blossomed like the strands of pink and white dogwoods lining the perimeter of the quad.

From a distance, Coach Stoltz was watching. "He really is an athlete."

36

Saturday morning at the McCaster home was purposely planned to be calm, a time to unwind from a productive week. On this particular morning, it was not to be. Andrew McCaster was the first to wake and picked up the phone beside the bed. The chaplain was on the receiving end of the call.

He was direct. "Did that boy get home last night?"

Cookie woke in time to hear the chaplain reply, "No, sir. I stayed until 0300. The neighbor said she would sleep on the couch. The daughter retired to her room after your son left, but I doubt she slept. Billy was able to reach her in a way that neither the neighbor nor I couldn't."

McCaster responded, "Billy said they had dated but I didn't know anything about that. Guess I will find out more later. I will send Billy back over to check on them at 0900. I need you to follow up at 1000 and then update me."

"Yes sir."

Andrew hung up the phone, and Cookie saw the concerned look on his face. "Take a shower, and I will put on a pot of coffee and make breakfast. Sounds like you and Billy will need it." She was empathetic toward Emily's current situation, but Cookie could still not let go of her impressions of her and her family. That would be another battle for another day.

She stopped by Billy's room and looked in the door. "You better get dressed. Gonna be a hard day."

As she finished the coffee and started the bacon, Andrew slipped behind her and gave her a warm embrace. They heard the shower start and before they finished their first cup, Billy appeared in his Levi's and a polo shirt. Cookie leaped into action and the three sat in silence as they wolfed down their eggs, bacon, and toast. As usual, Cookie and Billy awaited their orders.

"Billy, Cole still had not come home as of zero three hundred. I will need you to go check on the girl at zero nine hundred and the chaplain will return at ten hundred. Hopefully, the boy will be there. If he is not, start calling friends."

Commander McCaster noticed something different about Billy. Billy was genuinely concerned. It was as if he grew up overnight. There was a maturity about him now. Had he missed it somehow? Whatever caused this change in Billy, he hoped it wouldn't go away.

"Yes sir." Cookie and Andrew looked at each other as if to say, "*Who the hell is this kid?*"

Billy grabbed his keys and started toward the door. "I'll check in with you often. Can we take her some lunch later?"

Shit! "Yes, of course. I will make some chicken salad and there will be enough for them to eat off it for a few days."

"Thanks. I'll pick it up later."

Billy made his way to the car. He did not rev the engine and made his way to Emily. He arrived just before nine, and Janet greeted him at the door.

"She hasn't been out of her room, and Cole is still not here. Can you try to get her to eat something? I made some grits and toast. The grits are warm, but you might need to make some fresh toast. If you can stay for a while, I need to go home and freshen up."

"I am planning on it." Emily heard Billy's voice and opened her door as Janet closed the front door behind her.

"Emily, come get something to eat. You need to keep up your strength."

"OK. I am going to need a few minutes first. Can you call around and see if Cole is over at somebody's house spending the night or something?"

"I was planning on doing that already. I will put some bread in the toaster and get right on it."

While Emily showered and dressed, Billy called Pete and anyone else he thought Cole might have stayed with. He didn't think Cole was the kind of kid that would make friends easily, and he was ashamed of the way that he had treated Cole. Billy had hoped to redeem himself with Cole last week, but Cole had not attended school, and Cookie had him on lockdown. And there is the whole investigation by the principal. Nothing made sense to Billy as he was challenged to put together a theory. He had simply left him over at the creek by the school, and he didn't come home. Now he was gone again and Billy still had no clue. Nobody in Billy's limited circle knew anything, but they agreed to expand their reach. Nobody returned a call with new information.

Emily appeared as he finished his last call. Her eyes were still swollen. "Billy, I am glad we have some time alone. I do need to talk to you, but this is terrible timing. I have been upset for days now."

"I understand, Em. I mean your mom just died, and Cole is not back, yet. You have a lot on your plate." He realized that his delivery was cold and matter-of-fact. It was the way his dad would have said it and he couldn't help the way it came out.

"No Billy, it's not that." Her voice shook as she tried to tell him.

Billy embraced her. It was more loving than the comforting hug he had given her the previous night. "What is it, Emily? You can tell me anything. You know I love you, right?"

"But your mom. Oh, Billy, this is so hard."

"Are you breaking up with me? Please don't say that Emily. My mom doesn't get to pick who I love or…"

Emily interrupted him. "I will love you forever and I knew it from the first time we, you know…made love. At least it was love for me."

"It was for me, too. You are my first and only true love, Emily, and I can't lose you."

She allowed herself a deep breath and steadied her leaky voice as she finally delivered an apologetic message, "I'm pregnant."

"Oh, dear!" The young lovers turned to hear the door close and see Janet standing there in shock.

37

A million thoughts flooded Janet's mind. *Where is Cole? Was this why Ann chose to leave in a driving storm yesterday? Has she been drinking? Did Emily know about Ann's night in Charleston with that stranger? Why was Emily yelling at her?* She put all that aside and drew on her motherly instincts. *Just do the opposite of what Ann would do.*

"I didn't mean to eavesdrop, but I can't "unhear" it. You're getting a full helping of adult life dumped on you all at once. Just know that I'm here to support you through it however I can. Whatever you need, I will be available. I don't want to barge into your private matters, but just let me know if you need help." *This poor child. That boy!!!*

"We love each other." Billy was off to a good start, and Emily relaxed a little realizing he would not dump her. Janet heard the sincerity in his voice.

"Maybe I should leave you alone for a little while. I am next door if you need me." Before she left, she boldly asked "Who else knows?"

"Just us." Emily paused, "And you. Please don't tell anyone." She remembered her mom again and started to cry.

Billy wrapped his arms around her again and whispered "It's OK. It's OK. I'm here for you…and the baby."

Billy let it be known that all he wanted was to be with Emily and start their family. They were both nearly eighteen, and they could just run away together. "I can join the Navy when I turn eighteen in September. You turn eighteen before June so we can get married after you graduate. I don't know where we can live in the meantime. I mean my mom ..."

"I want to be with you too, Billy. The Navy sounds great for us. I won't be like my mother, but you have to finish high school."

Plans were haphazard and incomplete. They needed guidance. It would be difficult to navigate the next week, much less the next year. Billy was the first to say, "I have to tell my parents."

Emily stood frozen but realized that it had to be done. "Better get it over with."

38

Cole could feel it. Change was in the air. It started as they rode the crest of the storm into Charleston Friday afternoon. His mom left in a downpour. Now, on Saturday, Cole felt a gentle breeze at his back as he sat beside Chad on aluminum bleachers beside the home dugout. The first game was lost 3-2 on a fielding error by first baseman Andy Orr. Cole was nervous for his friend as he took the mound in the second game. Andy pitched a gem, striking out nine *Tigers* over seven scoreless innings and driving in all three runs with a blast in the 3rd. The team and cadets all seemed to have so much pride in the school, and Cole bought in. He was especially mindful of his new football coach. Coach Stoltz occupied the third base box for both games. He was knowledgeable, encouraging, and animated. It was apparent to Cole that he had earned the respect of not only the players, but the cadets, and attending faculty as well.

"Does the coach teach a class?" He directed his question to nobody in particular.

A twin seated in front of him turned and said, "Yes, he teaches social studies. He's my dad. My name is Carly and this is my sister, Sarah."

"I'm Chad and this is Cole." Like the other cadets, Chad had tried many times to steady his nerves to talk to them. They were seniors and he was just a sophomore. The girls knew he had money, but had long ago decided they would not entertain advances from anyone other than a senior. Without consulting Sarah, Carly had broken the pact when she talked to Cole. She had listened to his raspy voice for nearly fourteen innings now and was curious enough to learn more about the lean stranger with the odd smile.

"Yes, we know who you are Chad," as she gave him a dismissive look and directed her attention to Cole. "So are you a new cadet?"

"Maybe. I'm on a weekend visit and I have a tryout with your dad later." The breeze suddenly felt warmer. The attention seemed to close the deal. "If everything goes well with your dad, I can see me coming back in time for spring practice."

Carly was a little flustered. She had never considered an interest in someone younger than her. She liked the attention she got from the knobs next door at The Citadel. Cole seemed different. He sounded different. He looked more mature and spoke like he was a full-grown man. Cole was sixteen going on twenty-five. He had been quietly independent for years, preferring to be alone fishing, or in his room reading a book. It was painful to interact with his mom, and he had long sworn off yielding to the temptation of alcohol.

"Well, do y'all have plans for later?" Sarah nudged Carly's knee with a force that was a strong NO.

"We do." Chad also nudged Cole with his elbow with a force that said *I'll tell you why later.*

Cole was a quick learner and concluded that this was not the road to travel. He had formed a quick friendship with Chad and would not risk it for a pretty face. "Maybe another time."

The bleachers emptied and Chad told Cole to stay away from the coach's girls. "They like to party, but last year, a couple of boys on the team got drunk with them and were expelled. There was a rumor that Sarah even got pregnant and had an abortion. Maybe that was just a rumor. They are popular, and easy on the eyes, but not worth the drama. My dad always tells me to watch out for girls like that because they can ruin your life with an unwanted pregnancy. But they are so hot, right?"

"Yeah, very hot." Something stirred in Cole's loins and the breeze stiffened. He caught himself on the edge of embarrassment and refocused on his tryout. "Time to see the coach for the tryout."

The team had just broken the huddle in center field, and the boys scrambled to the shed adjacent to the concession stand. Coach Stoltz and the assistants barked orders.

"Outfielders, get the tarps and pins. Infielders, grab the rakes. Pitchers, load up the cart with clay and the tamp. Everybody hustle to your stations!"

Despite being the hero of the game, Andy was repairing the damage to the holes deepened by the cleats in front of the pitching rubber. He tamped down the dirt and teammates rolled out the tarp and nailed it down to cover the mound. Coach stepped off the John Deere and detached the screen from the back as he finished the field drag. Cole was mesmerized by the efficiency. Everyone had a job to do and the boys kept the field to the same standard as their rooms and uniforms. It was the last home game but the boys would practice one last time on Monday for their final game at Burke High School on Tuesday. He now turned his attention to Chad and Cole waiting for him on the sidelines.

Alec joined them, and the boys made their way to the football field. It was clear to Cole as he put on his cleats that Alec would be nothing like Billy. Although he was a rising senior like Billy, he didn't feel the need to jab anyone to compensate for any shortcoming of talent. He was a confident and polished QB and it rubbed off on Cole. He ran crisp routes against air and then against Chad. He and Alec had an instant connection. Chad had been penciled in as a starting DB next year. He earned it with hard work and was more than capable against the current receivers on the team. Cole proved to be more than he could handle, easily beating him on route after route.

Alec spoke privately to Coach and did not mince words. "We need him."

As they returned to the dorm, wind gusts from the north overtook the breeze, and the warmth of the air was replaced by a cool breath that whirled loudly as if calling a name, *Cole*.

39

The chaplain arrived at 10 hundred and Billy left at 1030 to talk with his parents.

"My mom is putting together some lunch. I should be back around noon."

The chaplain nodded as Billy went to give Emily a warm embrace and quick kiss goodbye. Then he stopped by to update Janet. After the update, Billy asked Janet if he could rehearse what he would say to his parents.

"Of course." She was feeling better about Billy now.

After a few botched attempts and some advice from Janet, he settled on a script. The drive home seemed quick and he arrived shortly before 11. He found Cookie in the kitchen preparing lunch for Andrew and the Levy family. Andrew was in a comfortable chair in the living room with a deep dive into the Saturday issue of *The Washington Post*. He heard Billy and immediately directed the conversation to Cole.

"Any news about the boy yet?"

"Nothing yet, Dad. The neighbor seems to think he is at a friend's house, but nobody that I talked to knows. Can you come in here for a second?" Billy knew it would take more than a second and he also knew that serious discussions always happened around the kitchen table.

"Well, this is going to be hard to talk about, but you always said to be direct when you have to deliver troubling news." He was already off-script. "Has Mom talked to you about Emily?"

"Now is not the time for this Billy. I have not talked to your father, but with all that's happened, I planned on it later after things settle a little." Cookie was stuck and she couldn't avoid it now. Before she could continue, Billy was determined to spill his news.

"Mom caught me at Emily's house last week. We had sex. I love her, Dad, and it wasn't our first time."

Cookie saw a different look on Andrew's face. He usually masked his emotions, being a career Navy man and all. She noticed his raised eyebrows indicating disappointment, but he had a wry smile that read like some primitive paternal pride.

"I am just going to say it. She is pregnant and I love her and I am going to marry her." Billy sat quietly as he heard his mother gasp.

"I knew it. I knew it. I told you what she was after."

"Cookie, calm down. It is done now so we need to handle this as a family." Andrew's smile had disappeared. "First, son, are you sure she is pregnant?"

"She wouldn't make it up, Dad, especially with what has happened. Her dad is gone, her mother is dead, and her brother is missing. She has been dealing with it alone, and she told her mom last night. She thinks Mrs. Levy was on her way here to see Mom."

"Oh, my God. That's a lot to unravel, Billy. Still, why weren't you more careful? You know about protection and all." Cookie was more practical now.

"Well, it just happened. I don't know."

Cookie knew it was a risk but she was determined to ask anyway. "Are you sure it is yours?"

Andrew and Billy gave her a scowl and Billy said, "She is not that kind of girl, mom. This is someone who is going to be in my life, our lives, for a long time. It is my child and I need you both to support me and help us make a good plan. I shouldn't have to remind you that she lost her mother *yesterday!*"

Andrew gave his son the '*Cool it with your mom*' look. "Well, we know now. Let's circle back to this later after we have had some time to digest it. Let's get through the tragedy first and find her brother."

"OK Dad, but this isn't going away and if I can give Emily something to hope for, it could help her now. I told her I would drop out after this year, and we would get married this summer, but she told me I needed to finish high school."

"And she is right." Andrew McCaster was a quick thinker and was already formulating a preliminary *schedule*.

"If you marry this summer, you can still go to summer school and take your senior English and math classes. You can move the remaining spring semester classes to the first semester and graduate in December. That gets you out just in time. Meanwhile, we will send Emily to Columbia and get a two-bedroom apartment with your sister. That will save everyone a little embarrassment. After all, this sort of thing is still frowned upon."

Billy had not thought of any of it. "But we won't be together. And I am not embarrassed."

Cookie liked the idea of Emily going away, even though she would still be attached to her family. "You can visit her on weekends when you are not busy, but school is a priority. I was so hoping for college, Billy."

Andrew threw out a line hoping Billy would take the bait. "People still go to college in these situations, but it is difficult. Have you thought of how you will support a family, Billy?"

"Yes, sir. I am planning on joining the Navy."

"Good grief!" Cookie remarked as she saw the wry smile return to Andrew's face.

40

"I'm back. I have chicken salad sandwiches and a vegetable tray." When Billy arrived, he saw the fruits of Janet's labors as the neighbors loaded the countertop with pies, cakes, a family meal from KFC, and a deli tray. Billy took the chicken salad directly to the refrigerator as he passed by the chaplain who had helped himself to a turkey sandwich and some chips.

"People have been so kind. Isn't that right, dear?" It was not as much a question as a lesson. Janet had a reassuring smile as she addressed the statement to the occupants in general.

Emily responded, "Yes, very kind. Word got out somehow and neighbors have been dropping things off all morning." It was Saturday and one could not derail southern hospitality, but the chaplain wished it could have been scheduled better so as not to arrive all at once.

Billy focused on Emily. "Have you eaten anything? You need to keep up your strength now." Billy almost added *'Because you are eating for two'* but he caught himself before he blurted it out for the chaplain to hear. "Let me make you a plate and we can eat first. What do you want?" Billy already had a chicken salad sandwich upon the insistence of his mom and he wasn't really hungry. That normally didn't stop him, so he was hoping for fried chicken but he would have what Emily wanted.

Emily glanced over the spread, and not wanting to hurt Billy's feelings she said, "How about a chicken salad sandwich?"

"Perfect."

After lunch, the search for Cole continued, but there were simply no clues and the chaplain eventually left the home to Billy and Janet. Janet greeted neighbors offering their condolences, and food was planned to get the family through the week. Everyone had a peace about Cole, as if Ann was reassuring them from beyond. They never considered any morbid outcome. Cole was always introverted, but he was mature and self-sufficient, too. Emily admired this about her brother. She argued with her mom, while Cole hibernated in his cocoon. She wished that on Friday she had been more like Cole. Perhaps her mom would still be alive. She had been too anxious about her news and now she felt that she rushed to tell her mom. She decided she would not repeat that with her father. As thoughts of the baby began to flood her mind, she became eager to return to Billy's warm embrace that she experienced before he left her that morning.

"Oh, Billy, did you tell your parents? I am sorry, my brain..."

"Yes. It wasn't as awkward, if that's the word, as I was expecting. Mom went a little haywire but Dad was in full Navy mode. He helped me think and actually added some things we had not thought of."

"Like what?"

Billy was careful to explain the summer school part and early graduation first. He moved on to his sister in Columbia. "And you could even take some classes if you wanted, you know, before the baby comes and all."

"So they want to hide me away and make it all disappear? Oh my God!"

"No, no. I've messed this up, sorry. Of course, I will be there every weekend...as your husband."

"And your parents approved of us getting married?"

"Well, they didn't disapprove. So yes, I think so,"

They worked through the logistics and hurriedly planned a late June wedding. Emily wanted it to be private with just his parents. The McCasters wanted the same. Mike and Cole would not attend.

41

On late Saturday afternoon, the buildings along the quad cast long shadows over the lawn in front of the barracks. The boys were tired from the baseball games, drills, and tryouts. They decided that another night of cards was in order. The outcome was largely the same in the first round before they adjourned to the dining room for dinner. Salisbury steak and roasted potatoes with brussels sprouts on the side. Cole was the only boy that ate the brussels sprouts, focusing on maintaining his athletic body. The boys returned to the dorm and after a few more rounds of spades, they retired to their room and quickly fell asleep.

Cole once again dreamed of fishing and recalled his new friendships and dreamed a little about Carly and Sarah. Cole woke up at his natural time on Sunday morning, which happened to coincide with the required wake-up time for all the boys at the Academy. The boys showered, put on their Sunday dress, and quickly made their way to breakfast, and then church.

Sunday school and church were mandatory for those that stayed on campus. Cole didn't mind. Church was a place where he could escape home and think without having to listen to all the arguing. He always attended with the family in Crane, but they hadn't yet attended church in Foster Creek. It was Mike Levy that organized it, and Ann Levy was a reluctant participant. She never talked to anyone and seemed to find the whole church scene fake.

The chapel at the Academy was large enough to hold the entire student body for school assemblies and a required Wednesday chapel service, but felt barren on most weekends. Chad noted that this particular weekend was more full than normal. Sunday school began promptly at 8:00 AM, followed by a 9:30 worship service. By 11:00, the boys were on the way back to their dorm, changed out of their Sunday dress uniforms, and then tidied up their rooms. There seemed to be a routine to everything, even on the weekends. Cole liked it. As the bell tower chimed its final note, it was noon, and the boys gathered again, then marched to the dining hall. They made their way to an abundance of parents waiting for their typical Sunday visitation and the much-anticipated and hyped fried chicken.

It was everything that the boys told Cole it would be. The chicken was double-dipped in buttermilk and floured after each dip. Deep-fried to a crisp and perfectly moist on the inside, Cole went for a thigh as he was accustomed to that piece. He smothered his chicken and biscuits with a thickened gravy made from the skimmed chicken crust and drippings that remained after each batch. Cole valued his vegetables, but he discarded the turnip greens and barely touched the candied sweet potatoes. Dessert was homemade peach cobbler a la mode, and Cole consumed two glasses of his cut tea to help wash it all down.

Cole spent the afternoon getting to know some of the parents of whom he was hoping would be his soon-to-be classmates. Coach Stoltz was there, but his twins were largely ignoring him. Cole noticed that their mom was not around and concluded that they must be divorced or something. Chad confirmed this and, for a moment, Cole felt sorry for the girls. He realized that his mom and dad didn't have a perfect marriage, either. They had little in common and argued all the time, but at least they were still married. He often wondered if they would be happier apart, but quickly set it aside knowing he would have likely gotten stuck with his mom. He couldn't imagine how and where they would have lived. The only skill he thought his mom had was drinking, and that led to the ongoing serious depression.

His dark thoughts led to a change in his climate. The afternoon would move along too quickly. He had less than twenty-four hours left before his mom returned. *Please let this work out.* He tried to cling to the sunshine for as long as he could. He thought of having to return to

Foster Creek High. He thought of Billy and Emily and their betrayal. Even Chad and the boys couldn't seem to divert his attention. He felt it. It was no longer the trailing breeze on which he wanted to coast. The wind whipped between the buildings, and he heard the voice again. *Cole.* A storm was indeed coming, and he knew he would be fighting a headwind now as he began to remember the details of the night he was held captive. He was definitely unprepared for the hurricane that he was about to encounter.

42

As Sunday morning rolled lazily into the afternoon, mild concern began to turn into widespread panic. Cole's whereabouts were still a complete mystery. With multiple officers tracking down even the weakest of leads, Cole could not be found. Law enforcement had been notified and meticulous plans were made to brief Mike Levy on the current situation as soon as he stepped off the boat in the Netherlands.

It was oh one twenty on Monday in the Netherlands and seventeen twenty at the Weapons Station. CWO Levy would soon catch a jumper on an Air Force cargo plane and arrive at 0840 at the Air Force base in North Charleston. He would arrive at his home at 0930 and control of the Cole situation would be passed off to Mike Levy. After Cole was found, funeral plans would be made, and the family notified. Mike was on a critical cruise, and it was not in the country's national interest to have him away from the nukes during routine maintenance. His absence left the sub vulnerable to being in a NATO port for too long.

Mike stepped off the sub and into the closest office. A phone was handed to him and Andrew McCaster briefed him. Chief Fiora had already delivered the blow about Ann. Mike was a military man and handled the death like a man that was trained not to show emotion. Besides, he lost feelings for her years ago. He was sad about what this meant to his kids, but he long suspected they were not close to their mom either. The drinking had ruined it for all of them.

He listened as if taking orders. "Yes, sir." He turned to the officer and asked, "I need to get to the Air Force base."

"We already have a driver waiting. They are holding the flight. We should be there in thirty minutes."

Levy turned, grabbed his duffle, and tossed it in the back of the jeep that pulled around while he was inside. "Let's roll."

The driver made good time and Mike thanked him as he drove him to the foot of the stairs. He was directed to the jumper seat and found a Marine hitching a ride for bereavement leave, as well. They had that in common, but neither said much during the six-hour flight. Mike tried to catch some shuteye as he was eager to get it all over with. His greatest hurdle would be how to manage the kids. His sister in Connecticut was plan A, a boarding school was plan B, and he had no plan C.

He had taken the optional life insurance policy for his spouse and children. With Ann's passing, the kids would split $50,000. Mike had socked away every bonus he ever received, and he made Ann live like a pauper. They lived modestly by his design and he decided that after funeral expenses, the funds would be doled out to his sister if she agreed to take them. Otherwise, Cole had two years of high school somewhere and Emily had planned to go on to college. He reviewed his plans again and drifted off somewhere over the Atlantic.

The plane hit a headwind that delayed their landing by ten minutes. A car was again waiting on him at the foot of the exit ramp. The drive from the base on Dorchester was only fifteen minutes to the house. The school had been notified of everything that happened, and they were put on alert to contact the chaplain immediately if they had news on Cole. Mike entered his home at 0930 as scheduled, and Emily ran to him as the tears began to flow.

"Dad, thank God, you're home." She wanted to say more, but she could tell her dad was in his own orbit and, as usual, there was no room for her. *I need to tell you about my last conversation with Mom. I want to tell you about Billy. We should talk about Cole.*

"You look exhausted. Why don't you go rest and let me catch up with the chaplain."

Mike outlined his plans for the funeral and his kids with the chaplain. He would need to talk to both at the same time so it was a waiting game now. "Where is that boy?"

43

After a quick goodbye to his daughters following Sunday lunch, Coach Stoltz met with Mr. Monroe. He had expected to exaggerate Cole's athletic prowess a bit, but was so genuinely impressed that the words came easy. Coach knew Cole was valued and if there was any way it could happen, his word would carry a lot of weight.

It was business now. "OK, Coach. So he gets a discount for the military and an athletic scholarship. You know, I'll have to run it by Mr. Russell."

"Of course. Being that he and Chad are becoming friends, I don't see a problem."

In addition to being Chad's dad and a major donor to the school, Sam Russell managed the large endowment that was used to fund all scholarships at the Academy. In fact, he managed the assets of The Citadel's endowment and those of most of the wealthier families of Charleston.

Mr. Monroe said he would get things started first thing in the morning. He expected Ann would be elated. They agreed that Cole seemed to enjoy his visit and anticipated a quick acceptance of the offer. Coach wanted him in time for spring football practice.

"I will call his school tomorrow morning when Mrs. Levy comes to get Cole. I should have an answer for you by noon. He seems to be a focused kid so he probably will not have much trouble adapting to our rigor. After they leave, I'll try to get some information about classes and check if there are any red flags. I can't fax a transcript request until he is officially enrolled, but I can usually finesse things a bit to get him set up in the right classes."

Mr. Monroe contacted Sam Russell first thing Monday morning. He was not surprised that he would get the go-ahead, but he was surprised that Mr. Russell would give such an enthusiastic endorsement. As it turns out, Chad had learned a little about networking from his parents and had already greased the wheel when he called his father late Sunday afternoon. Sam let his son practice his skills and gave varying viewpoints and counters, just to help Chad practice but, in reality, he was impressed with Cole, too.

Mr. Monroe had Cole follow Chad's class schedule on Monday. Cole was anxious and unsettled from a restless sleep, but Mr. Monroe's assurance settled him down. Cole decided to focus on what was right in front of him and not think too far ahead.

Coach saw him in the hall between classes and asked him, "Are you excited, Cole?

"Yes, but I am a little nervous. Should I go to the office at eleven?"

"No, they will send for you after Mr. Monroe has a chance to go over details with your mom. I have recommended a very good package for you."

"Package?"

"Financial aid. We just call it a package. I know Mr. Monroe is working on getting it finished to present to your mom."

"Thank you, Coach, for a great weekend and for the tryout. I hope it works out but…"

"No buts. Think positively. If you want to be here, we will make it happen."

The chimes came and went at eleven and when the single chime rang out at 11:30, Mr. Monroe decided to call Foster Creek High. He didn't like being idle and although he intended to wait on Ms. Levy, he hated wasting time. He looked through his Rolodex and dialed the number. A parent volunteer transferred him to the guidance office.

"Yes, ma'am, this is Paul Monroe over at Bishop Porter Academy. We have Cole Levy here finishing his weekend visit and…" Mr. Monroe was unaccustomed to being interrupted but he heard an alarming voice on the other end of the line.

"*You* have Cole. Mr. Monroe, his family has been looking for him all weekend. His father called this morning. I am afraid I have some terrible news. Cole's mother was killed in an automobile accident late Friday afternoon."

"Oh no." Mr. Monroe was at a loss as shock registered in his voice. "Do I need to call his father? Cole's visit was a little sudden and we didn't get an emergency number. Do you have it?

"Yes. Please call him. The number is 803-558-5756."

"Thank you, ma'am."

Mr. Monroe picked up the phone and dialed the Levy home. Emily answered and handed the phone to her father.

"Mike Levy." Military mode. Mr. Monroe was used to it.

After listening to Mr. Monroe, Emily heard her father say, "I know where that is. Please don't tell Cole what has happened. We can be there in an hour."

Emily felt a little lighter now as she moved silently to her room to ready herself for the difficult task of hearing her dad tell Cole about their mom's death. As she heard the click of the receiver she asked, "Where is he?"

"At some boarding school. Ann took him."

Go⸱, Mom!!!!

44

Alan Jaymes spent his weekend with a minor adjustment to his usual routine. He planned a stop by Blockbuster on Rivers Avenue and then a few miles' drive to North Charleston to an ABC package store beside the local Winn-Dixie. He rarely stopped at a liquor store close to where he worked, but this one was far from the school and base. Ever searching for approval, he had run into his nephew and a friend at the liquor store the previous weekend at about the same time. His nephew asked Alan to help him get some liquor. Mr. Jaymes had remembered a time when he could buy liquor at eighteen and decided it was harmless. A fifth of what $10 could buy, and Mr. Jaymes delivered it discreetly to the boys waiting in the car.

Now a week removed, Alan was not surprised to find the boys parked and waiting in the car. *At least they are smart enough to park closer to the grocery store this time.* As Mr. Jaymes parked his Tercel beside the boys, he saw his nephew, Morgan, rolling down the window.

"Y'all didn't get in trouble last week did you?"

"Nah. We just hung out by the lake and drank a little. Ran into a football kid from over at your school around nine and had a couple of drinks, then dropped him off."

"Well, just don't do anything stupid or tell anybody where you got this. You know your dad would kill me, right?"

"But you're cool, Uncle Alan. We would never rat you out. You know what it's like right? You must've partied all the time at our age."

"Oh yeah. My bros and I partied all the time." He took the ten-dollar bill Morgan had slid across the car door trim. "Same thing?"

"How about vodka this week?"

"Be right back." Alan Jaymes returned within minutes and slipped the brown paper bag to Morgan. "Look, it probably needs to be the last time. If something were to happen..."

"Nothing will happen. I will call you next week." Morgan started his Olds Cutlass and sped recklessly out of the lot.

Realizing his stumble, Mr. Jaymes shook his head before making his way home to a damp, drafty apartment in the basement of a Georgian estate home on Folly Road about a mile from The Citadel.

Morgan and his friend were stopped by the Foster Creek Police Department that Friday evening. While hauled away in the back of a patrol car, the boys watched as the red Cutlass was hitched to a tow truck. Morgan was more concerned about his car than his circumstance. After booking, reality set in and he had no choice but to call his father to bail him out. As the superintendent of schools drove him home early Saturday morning, Morgan did not keep his promise to Alan Jaymes.

"How did you get alcohol to begin with?"

"Alan gets it for us."

"*Gets* it for you! What? That sounds like this has happened before. How many times has my idiotic nephew done this?

"Just two. It won't happen again."

"Damn straight it won't. That's it. I'm done with him."

Superintendent Jaymes would call the principal at Foster Creek Monday morning and give him the good news, Alan Jaymes would not be rehired for the following year.

45

Emily and her father's drive from Foster Creek eerily mirrored that of her brother and mom just three days earlier. There was little conversation, and Mike Levy was treating everything as a box on a checklist of tasks he had to complete to fulfill his current mission. Emily stared blankly out the window as they drove down the interstate. Her thoughts were not so much of her mom and Cole as much as her future. She even allowed herself to fantasize about the perfect life she was going to make with Billy and their child. Her trance was broken as they finally turned into the long drive that led to the school.

She broke the silence, "This is beautiful. Is this where Cole is?"

"Apparently so." He pulled the car into a visitor's spot. "You can come in, but just listen."

They entered the administration building and eventually found Mr. Monroe. He did his best to explain what he knew, but could not offer any explanation to Mr. Levy as to *why* Cole was there. Emily could have cleared that up, but she chose to follow orders as she sat motionless. *Cole can tell you why, Dad!*

Mr. Monroe had an eerie feeling that Mike Levy couldn't care less about what had happened to his wife. After offering genuine condolences, he explained the details of the visit and offered support as a school family.

" We hope Cole will still consider making us part of his plans."

The scholarships were explained and an apology for the timing of all of it was extended. While he was digesting a flood of information,

Mike began to think that perhaps his plan B should become his plan A. He would talk to Cole about it privately later.

The most daunting task on the to-do list was now upon him. Mike Levy waited patiently while Mr. Monroe sent for Cole. Cole left the school and was still in his uniform, accompanied by Chad, as they made their way across the quad. They were not expecting a uniformed boy so it took a while to realize it was Cole,

Emily broke protocol. "Is that Cole? Who is that with him?"

Mr. Monroe responded, "That *is* Cole and he is with Chad. Chad was his host this weekend, and they have become fast friends. In fact, Cole seems to have made several friends here. Mostly with our athletes, but I saw a couple of the female cadets talking to him at the baseball game yesterday, too."

"Cole?" Emily could feel a grimace on her father's face. "Sorry."

"Did he buy those? Does he have other clothes?"

"No sir, we give all of our cadets the necessary uniforms when they enroll and we provide loaners for extended visitations. Cole's uniform is a loaner for now but under the circumstances, he can just wear it home. I will send Chad to get his other belongings while you talk to Cole."

Cole was excited to tell his mom of the opportunity he had earned. He would privately brag about the tryout. He would talk about Chad and his new friends. Most of all, he would insist that she allow him to enroll immediately. He had decided that he would ask Mr. Monroe when he could start. He needed to emphasize that he wanted to be part of spring football practice. He would tell his mom he would not return to Foster Creek High, so she might as well approve this. She should. After all, it was her plan.

Chad opened the heavy, glass-paneled door and Cole made eye contact with his father. *This can't be good. He is supposed to be gone for at least another two months. And Emily is here too. Something must have happened to Mom.*

"Dad, where is Mom?"

"Son, I have some very bad news."

Deep down, Cole already knew. He felt his life change in the shifting winds all weekend. She had come to him in the wind, steadying him for this moment. He became numb and inattentive as his father methodically explained the details of his wife's death.

Another box was checked for Mike Levy. The most difficult box. The list of tasks was getting smaller, but the thing about a checklist is that when one box is checked, another one surfaces and becomes a new priority.

Cole was mournful now mostly because he knew he would have to leave for a while. He hoped that his dad would act decisively and put all this behind them. He could not imagine a better alternative than the academy. Dark thoughts were raging from deep within.

I hate Foster Creek. Dad has never been there for us. Does he know about Emily and Billy? Does he know what happened to me in the woods? Would he even care? Mom was the only one that even tried. I just can't...

"After things get settled at home, Dad, can I come back here?" Cole was empty again, but his rasp was steady and he was yet to form a tear. He would not cry again for years. He always acted cold, but his withdrawal from reality was magnified when something bad happened. He had inherited it from his father.

"We will keep it as an option. I will circle back to it later. I have to make final arrangements for your mom now."

Mike Levy checked another box while striking a line through *plan A*.

46

News about Cole's mom spread like wildfire at the Academy. The card-playing crew was especially distraught. Alec even came up to check on the boys from the second floor. He was hopeful of Cole joining the team, but everyone had doubts now. Mr. Monroe had assured Chad that Cole expressed a desire to come back, and the boys just needed to exercise some patience. Chad called home and told his parents of the surreal events of Cole's mom who was already dead while he was visiting all weekend. Mr. and Mrs. Russell told Chad they would offer any help they could for Cole and his family. After comforting Chad, Sam Russell called the school to get the number to the Levy home. Moments later, the phone rang on Sunset Drive.

"Mike Levy."

"Mr. Levy, my name is Sam Russell and my son Chad goes to Bishop Porter. He was Cole's host this weekend. We are all very sorry for your loss."

"Well, thank you very much. We are making arrangements now." This was not on Mike Levy's to-do list and his tone was dismissive.

Mr. Russell wasn't going to be dismissed that easily. "Chad and the boys are in shock. I just want you to know that we already think a lot of Cole. He made a great first impression and he and my son became fast friends. Please let us know if we can do anything to help y'all."

Mike recognized a sincerity in Sam's voice. Funeral is looking like Wednesday at 1400 at the chapel on base."

"If it is not too much, we would like to bring Chad and show our support for Cole."

"Well, there will be plenty of room. Ann was a loner and we've only been here since January. We are at the Weapons Station in Foster Creek. I will have to put your name on the list at the gate. Did you say 'Sam Russell?'"

"Yes, my wife is Betty. And, of course, Chad and maybe a couple of other cadets, but I don't know yet."

"No problem. I really just need the adults and a count. I'll put down 5 just in case. Do you want to speak with Cole?"

Mr. Russell was not intending to, but he wouldn't dodge it either. "That would be great if he is up to it."

"He is taking this well. He has never worn his emotions on his sleeve much and this is no different. He already said he wants to go back to the Academy, but we haven't talked about it yet. The logistics are a little tricky. I have a daughter about to graduate, so it's not just about Cole. But maybe, if we can work it out. He seemed to be happy when I first saw him. Of course, that was before we told him about his mom. Cole, telephone!"

Cole called downstairs, "Who is it? I don't want to talk..."

"It's Mr. Russell, Chad's father." Mike heard the heavy feet from Cole's room as he hurried through the door and pounded the stairs. He took the phone from his dad and stretched the ten-foot cord into the hallway.

"Hello, this is Cole."

Mike Levy saw a spark in his son as he observed the conversation. Cole still lacked emotion, but his posture improved. There were telltale signs that Mr. Russell could help. As Cole seemed to be wrapping things up, Mike gestured that he wanted to speak to him again.

"My dad wants to talk to you again if that is OK."

"Of course, Cole. Take care and we will see you Wednesday."

"Mike Levy again. I won't keep you long. Earlier, you said you were willing to help. Could we talk a little after the funeral? It's about one of those logistical hurdles."

"Yes, of course. I meant it when I said we would like to help. See you Wednesday. Bye."

Sam found it odd that Mike pivoted so easily. He found it more odd that nobody seemed to be grieving. *Everyone grieves differently. I would be lost without Betty and I know Chad would cry for a week. There is something in the shadows with that family.*

Mike planned the funeral and it was purposefully simple. Ann's body would be cremated after the viewing. She had no siblings and her parents died before they first met in San Diego.

Mike had long concluded that she was desperate after her parents died. He remembered being drawn to her auburn hair as well as her vulnerability, and he stepped right into her snare in San Diego. He always knew that she trapped him with the pregnancy. Emily was an anchor baby for a Navy man. Mike was at sea when he decided on a divorce. When he returned to deliver the blow, Ann strengthened her hold on him with the unexpected pregnancy of Cole. Still, he had planned to leave once the baby was born, but once he heard "It's a boy!" all bets were off.

Tuesday turned into Wednesday morning before Mike was ready to listen to Cole. They drove to a park and got comfortable on a bench. Cole felt the warmth of sunshine on his face. Then with the message his father delivered, he felt a surge of relief and excitement. Cole quickly decided now was not the time to express too much excitement given his mother's passing. Pending a conversation with Mr. Russell, Cole would be able to start at BPA on Monday.

"Can I start tomorrow?"

47

"Blessed are those who mourn, for they will be comforted."
Matthew 5:4

The Navy chaplain quoted the verse. A violinist played *Amazing Grace*. It was a nice service, but nobody mourned the deceased. The hymn didn't soften Mike Levy as he affirmed the *wretch-like-me* part as it pertained to Ann.

Navy personnel filled the Joint Base Chapel in support of Mike and the kids. The McCasters were there. There was an awkwardness when Billy sat beside Emily. Janet was there, but none of the other ladies that helped lead Ann to her demise with their gossip were in attendance. Somewhere near the back, the Russells were seated along with Andy and Tegan. Cole acknowledged them and for a moment, their presence helped him forget his anger toward Billy. There was still a lot for Cole to unpack. His thoughts were his burden, and they were so scrambled, he scarcely heard what was said about his mom.

As the service ended, the officers that worked closely with Mike shook his hand and greeted Emily and Cole as the procession left the chapel. Janet soon followed and was especially attentive to Emily. She gave her a quick wink as she left and made her way to Billy and his family on the front lawn.

"Hello, I am Janet. I live next door to Ann."

"Oh yes, we've met," Cookie reluctantly acknowledged. She had discarded her like she had Ann, leaving them to form their own little clique.

"Mom, she is helping take care of Emily. She knows about us. We are telling her dad tomorrow." Billy wanted her mother to be nicer to Janet. Cookie was not completely heartless. Maybe Janet could help her get rid of this little problem.

Cookie pounced, sizing Janet up to be too stupid to follow. "That is nice of you to help. Emily sure stepped knee-deep into it, but this is not the time."

Same bitch as before. "No, not the time. Billy, let me know if y'all need anything. Remember what we talked about," as she scoffed at Cookie and turned away.

Andrew didn't want a scene. "What is this about?"

Billy said, "I'll tell you later, Dad. Like mom said, 'not the time.'"

Billy turned toward Emily and saw a well-dressed man and his wife lingering at the end of the line. Three boys his age were in their formal cadet dress blues. As they greeted Cole, Mr. Levy dismissed his children. While Cole and the boys went off to the garden beside the chapel, Emily boldly made her way toward Billy and his parents.

Cookie pretended that she didn't notice, speaking loud enough for Emily to hear, "There's Sandy. I am going to say hello." She waved in the general direction of a lady she barely knew and strolled casually away.

"Mr. McCaster, I am Emily. Thank you for coming and thank you for the advice, too."

He was unaccustomed to being called anything but Commander McCaster but found the mistake innocent enough. "No problem. Billy says you are planning on speaking to your father about the situation tomorrow."

"Yes, that's right. Cole is probably going away to school with those boys. I think they are his new friends." They looked over and Cole and the boys were talking, smiling, and laughing.

Billy was more aware now and seemed a little jealous. "Seems like it. I like Cole but I really screwed it up. I hope we can straighten things out one day."

Commander McCaster was puzzled. "What do you mean, Billy?"

Emily was not yet ready for that. "I don't think he was happy about me and Billy. He doesn't know yet, but he didn't like that I was dating one of his friends, I guess."

Andrew seemed to accept the explanation. "I see. Well, I am going to let you talk for a while. Billy, come find us in about ten minutes."

"Yes sir."

The Russells listened as Mike signed off on Cole attending the school. He had one simple request, if they could look in on Cole when they looked in on Chad.

"I have to report back to my boat. It is a matter of national security. In some ways, the school is a blessing for Cole and me."

Betty was a concerned mother. "What will your daughter do?"

Mike explained that he and Janet had spoken and Emily would finish high school living with her, then enroll and start college in the summer term. He would check on both his kids when he was in port or on leave.

Sam Russell gave some assurances. "Of course. We had already planned to have him come home with Chad for some deep-sea fishing. We can help him navigate this. Chad can use a good friend this summer. He can even come stay with us when you are not here."

"Cole does love fishing. I know he'll be in good hands. After we settle the estate, Cole will get a small amount of money. He probably will want a car. He has his license but we just couldn't manage a car yet."

"I get it. We haven't got Chad one yet either."

"I just don't want him to waste the money. Maybe save it for college."

"Well, I manage money for a living. As a matter of fact, I manage funds for the school endowment and I would be more than happy to advise Cole, if you like."

"Well, that would be great."

Mike was running out of boxes to check.

48

Eager to resume his life, Mike approved Cole's request and called Mr. Monroe, and explained the current status. Mr. Monroe worked quickly. He called Foster Creek and obtained current grades and classes. He scheduled most of Cole's core classes with Chad and moved Chad to the downstairs suite that he would share with Cole. By 0730 Thursday, Cole was welcomed back by Mr. Monroe and Chad. Cole insisted that he start classes that very day, and stopped by his new digs and dropped off his belongings. By 0800 he was sitting in his first period.

Mr. Monroe explained to Cole that they did not offer *Mechanical Drawing* but would give him credit as an elective. He would have to replace it with *Current Events.* Cole was very happy to learn that his only class without Chad was *World History,* and the schedule listed Stoltz as the teacher. He battled thinking of Mr. Jaymes, a loose thread to remind him of his recent trauma. He liked his new coach. As he made his way through the day, his mind settled as he followed his new routine.

After Mr. Levy signed the admissions papers and award offer, he was given a very brief tour of the campus. He made quick time as he drove home against the traffic. His thoughts on the drive were all business. He was task-oriented now and like Cole, he was largely void of emotion. He would now wrap things up with Emily. He was decisive and his mind could not be changed. *Emily will agree to the plan to stay with Janet and start college this summer.* He would encourage a dorm room, but she could get an apartment with her share of the proceeds from the life insurance policy. It was his last box, and he needed Emily to cooperate and accept the plan. She would accept parts of his plan, but for reasons he did not yet know.

Emily was up and waiting on her father when he returned. Unlike the cries for her Mom when Ann returned from the Academy, she remained silent. She was more upset about saying goodbye to Cole than her mother's death. The cumulative effect of everything was testing her resilience. She had wondered about her obligations as an older sister. But now that Cole was safe, few obstacles remained to block her life with Billy.

Mike asked his oldest child to sit at the table as he awkwardly tried to make a cup of coffee. He could scarcely tolerate the clutter. "What a mess. Let's get rid of all this crap today."

"It's Mom's crap and I want to keep some of it."

Mike had no attachment to anything Ann. "Fine, but put it in a box and stow it away in your room."

Emily connected her thoughts and concluded that they would be on the move. She had hoped to have the talk with her dad today but not the instant he came home. "Dad, I need to…"

Mike anticipated something unsolicited and he quickly redirected. "Emily, we need to talk about options. I will lay them out for you and since you are eighteen soon, I will let you decide. Cole is at the boarding school now, so it's just you and me. As you know, my job is critical. I actually ship out on Sunday."

It was a lie. Commander McCaster had given him two weeks. Emily already heard as much from Billy.

"These are the options I have for you. I have spoken to the neighbor, Janet. She has agreed that you can stay with her until you graduate. She insisted. You can enroll in college somewhere if it's not too late and start summer classes. The Navy has staff that will help you with those logistics."

"Well, I like the part about living with Janet until I graduate but…"

"To be honest, the only other option is to go live with my sister in Connecticut, but that means transferring to a new high school."

"I've had enough of moving schools. I will stay with Janet."

"Have you thought about what college you would attend, or maybe join the Navy?"

"Dad, to be honest, I don't see college as an option now. Mom had me apply to Charleston Southern, but I need to get further away. But I do see the Navy in my future. Can I think about this more and talk with you later?"

She had not lied, she was going to be part of a Navy family. It is all she had known. She would serve her country by supporting Billy and raising their child.

"Yes, later. In the meantime, I will go get some boxes. I have a few errands. I will have movers come Monday and move the furniture and boxes to storage. Gonna need to find an apartment when I get back. Something nice off-base this time." Mike was less selfish now. His kids suffered as Ann trimmed the food budget to support her drinking problem. Their kids had eaten cereal and sandwiches most days of their life. Dinner was minimal unless Mike was home. Mike Levy knew it.

Emily bit her tongue. *You want a nice apartment now? Of course. Never for us, never for Mom. No wonder she was so miserable.* "I'll start sorting through things while you are gone."

"Just your things. I need to go through the crap. You can take what I don't want to keep."

"Yes, sir!" Emily stared through him. *At least Mom tried to be nice. Did you ever love me?* As she reached her room, she heard the sound of the squeaky wheels disappearing as the car rolled around the corner.

49

Hours had passed and Emily had no warning of her father's arrival. One of Mike's errands was to pick up the check from State Farm for the minivan. He always hated it and used the check to replace it that very day with something more suitable for a single man. He was always practical but refused to act on the recommendations of nearly everyone, including *Consumer Reports*, and opted instead for a 1988 Pontiac Firebird. He was old school, not yet ready to buy the hype of an Asian import.

Emily heard the car door slam and stopped the purge of her belongings. She saw him open the trunk and pull out the unassembled moving boxes. "You got a new car?"

"Yes, I turned the loaner in and I used the insurance money from the minivan to get it."

"Was that van worth *that* much?"

Mike Levy thought it to be none of her business but decided to throw her a bone. "Well, no, but there was a death benefit also. That covered it all with a little to spare. You know your mom had a life insurance policy, just a small one really. She named you and Cole as the beneficiaries. Should be settled in a couple weeks. After we pay for the funeral costs, you should get about $20,000 each."

Emily was shocked to hear it. Mike knew it would squash any objection to his new ride. "That was nice of her, Dad."

"*Her!* I am the one that paid the damn premiums on it."

Emily was constantly reminded of how calloused her father was. She was glad she would be rid of him soon. She loved him because he was her dad, but she never liked him. And he had always resented her. She looked like her mom. Maybe that was why he never really trusted her.

"Is that it then? Are you washing your hands of us now?"

"That is a cruel thing to say." Deep down, he knew she was right. "The money can't bring her back, but it can be used to help you better your life. You've been forced to be an adult since you were fourteen. In some ways, you are more ready to move forward than me or Cole."

"So the money thing is set in stone now?"

"Yes, it is a legal thing. Beneficiaries can't be changed, and I wouldn't try even if I could. I don't really need the money."

His tone was harsh. It had been for days, cold as the icy driveway in Crane. And now he was gloating. Emily decided she had nothing to lose now. Mike's mind seemed made up and the moves he was making revolved mostly around only his own well-being. She had to look after herself now. Her future was now more secure, so she would say it in a way to hurt him. She had not learned her lesson with her mother. He could not trump her. The final say would be hers.

"Dad, I am not going to school this summer. I am marrying Billy McCaster and he is joining the Navy next fall. And…I'm pregnant."

She had victory. He had no power over her now. She fired her bullet. She had no clue that her dad had a bazooka, and he fired its rocket right into her heart.

"Just like your mother."

Finally, she wept.

50

As they packed the house, Mike Levy used the silence to reflect on his choices. His life would be different now. When he told his own father about how Ann trapped him, his dad told him, "You can't choose a life now, you can only live one."

For the first time in his life, Mike *did* have choices. Emily had complicated things by this unexpected pregnancy and circumstances were further amplified by the awkwardness of Billy being his boss's son. Even so, things seem to be falling into place for Mike Levy. He would see Cole when he could and Emily, well, she was leaving and he was angry. He made his choices long ago. His career was always number 1. Supporting his family was part of the life he had to live. That was number 3. He had worked, planned, and socked away money for the day he walked away from them. That was his number 2. Cole was always his reason for staying, but as Cole grew older, Mike became more distant from him, too.

Some families exist just to exist. They are layered and when one peels away enough skin, what is sometimes exposed is messy. What held this family together was thin like thread. Thread can be braided into twine. and twine braided into a strong rope. The Levys never learned how to make cordage. They all just lived a life. Ann took the easy way out. She didn't see any way to save them. It took her tragedy to turn the fortunes of Mike and the kids. They all had hope now. The cords were cut, and the thin ties that bound them unraveled.

They finished packing Saturday afternoon, and the house was silent like death. The tension between them was taut. A dreary mood was setting in, and Mike refused to let it take hold of him. He was leaving in the morning and mostly to help himself, he broke the silence.

"So where will you and *Billy* live until he graduates? The McCasters?" *I hope not.*

She didn't want to talk, but his words eased her anxiety a little. "I am moving to Columbia and staying with Billy's sister until the baby is born. We will go to boot camp in December and then who knows. I'll keep up with Cole. He can update you if you want to know."

"I see." Still angry, he at least knew she would not be thrown to the street. "And when is this wedding? You know it is difficult with Billy being my Commander's son and all."

"Yes, I know that. Just going to elope or something I think. Nothing formal at all. You don't need to do anything. Billy's dad is advising us."

"I see." *So Billy's dad is helping you and Chad's dad is going to help Cole. What they must think of us. Fuck it, I need to get out of here.*

"Do you have what you need over at Janet's now?"

"Yes, just waiting on Billy to help me move my bed."

"Well, I am going to go ahead and head out then." He was eager now. The last boxes were ready to go and so was he. He had accomplished his mission and now it was time to forget. It was his time to choose a life.

"I thought you didn't leave until tomorrow." She didn't really care.

"Yeah, well, I have already taken down the bed and put the mattresses in dust covers for storage. I heard you call Billy and ask him to help you move your bed, so I went ahead and got a room close to the base. Should be back on the sub by 20 hundred tomorrow, local time."

He was fumbling for his keys as he spoke. These were his final words to her. She saw him reach for his duffle as he opened the door.

"Bye, Dad." And she heard the door close behind him.

Mike Levy arrived at the Dorchester Inn around seventeen thirty on Saturday evening. He set his alarm for an early wake-up call, expecting to quickly fall fast asleep. He picked up the phone and dialed the number given to him by Mr. Monroe.

A mannerly lady answered, "Sumter Dorm, this is Ms. Fields. How can I help you?"

"This is Mike Levy. I was told I could call my son, Cole, at this number. Can I talk to him, please?"

"This is the correct number, but Cole went home with Chad this weekend. The log indicates they plan to be back tomorrow for lunch. It's fried chicken. He is such a nice young man. Can I have him call you tomorrow or do you have the Russell's number?"

So I guess this is it then. I really am alone now.

"No, but that is fine. I'll try him again when I am able. Tell him I called, please."

"Certainly. Anything else?"

"No, bye."

He felt completely alone now and found it difficult to sleep. He decided to exercise his new freedom and put on fatigues and made his way downstairs. At the bar, he struck up a conversation with a pretty blond half his age. He knew her intention, but he was experienced now. Twenty minutes later, he was laying with her in his hotel room. It had been a while but it came back to him quickly. *'A girl in every port'* was not far from the truth, and he fantasized about all the women he could have now. This time around, he was experienced and more disciplined. Most of all, he will always be prepared. Ann was in his past, and he vowed not to let history repeat itself.

51

After his first night as a cadet, Cole awakened to the sound of Chad's alarm. He followed Chad's routine and readied himself for the day. Inspection came and went and the boys packed up their books and made their way to breakfast. On the quad, swaths of sunshine lapped the savory dew as the long morning shadows cast by the buildings and lingering pines surrendered their posts. Cole moved seamlessly through his day. He was more alive now. As his day passed, he took more notice of his surroundings. He soaked in the finer details of his new digs. Every hour was different. The campus seemed to be painted with a cool, calming palette of color in the morning. When the shadows yielded, the bright stone administration building reflected the sunlight, and Cole felt bright and alert.

By the time classes ended on his first Friday, Cole was eager to go with Chad. He was eager to allow himself the possibility of forgetting the life *he* led. As Chad's mom drove the boys through the patchy shade that flooded the long driveway, Cole turned and noticed the warm hues of the campus painted by the dimming of the day. This was home now.

The Russells lived on James Island and were equidistant to the Charleston peninsula and the high-end beach and golf resorts on adjacent islands. The home was a large Georgian and it backed right up to the marsh with its various estuaries. It was a large waterfront estate home and it sat on a lush and well-manicured lot. The boxwoods that lined the drive and the full azaleas and tropicals in the beds around the home put all the houses on the base to shame. The driveway seemed polished but it was just a well-cleaned and maintained white concrete. As they pulled just short of the garage, Cole noticed the pool and a hot tub spilling over into a small garden pool that spit a fountain of water back into the swimming pool. There were wooden barrels of flowers in bloom that seemed almost out of place this early in spring. The boys exited and made their way up the back stairway of the home and entered a large screened-in porch with a magnificent view of the marsh. The added height now revealed the dock, the boat, and the meandering water that lead to the more distant Intracoastal waterway.

Cole was drawn to the water first. "Can you fish off your dock?"

"Of course, we can do it tomorrow. Do you like to swim?"

"Yes, but I didn't..."

The Russells were committed to their promise to Mike Levy. "Cole, I took the liberty to buy you a few things to keep here, like some swim trunks and sandals. Boys like to pick out their own hats so we can go to the surf shop down the street and pick one out tomorrow. I insist."

It was pointless for Cole to refuse it. He just kept it simple. "Yes ma'am. That is very thoughtful of you."

"And if there is anything else..."

"You've done more than enough, thank you. I have some shorts and stuff I brought with me. I may need some sunscreen though."

"I bet you burn easily. So do I, and we always have sunscreen on hand. I can't get Chad to use it. He is like his father. They just tan."

"I am more like my mom. Well.."

There was an awkward moment of silence. Chad nudged Cole. "Let me show you to our room. He guided Cole up a back stairway to a large room with twin beds on each side.

"This is my room. That's your bunk by the window."

The Russell home had a smaller bunk room down the hall to accommodate Chad's friends. There were also two more formal guest rooms for visiting adults. In the rear center of the 2nd floor, an open area housed a large console TV and a video player. There was a piano and guitar, and in front of a large picture window, Mr. Russell's desk overlooked the expansive marsh views. The downstairs contained the

Russells' suite, a library, a formal living room, a dining room, the family room, and a half bath. The ceilings were 10-feet tall and a large glass-paneled front door opened onto a veranda furnished with wicker and tropical plants. It would take Cole some time to get his bearings. He had never seen anything like it. Everything was clean and organized and on a grand scale. There was no clutter or mess like at his house. *This is the life.*

As they sat in the kitchen, Betty played it down as she saw the glazed look in Cole's eyes. It was not the first time Chad had awestruck friends from the Academy visit. She knew how to downplay their wealth. "Mr. Russell works very hard."

Cole wanted to know more. "What does he do?"

"Financial advisor." Chad cut him off. "He will tell you more later if you want. He should already be here. Where is he, Mom?"

"He called. He was doing a favor for someone. Wait, I think that's him now. Sam?"

"Yes, it's me." He kissed his wife and ruggedly hugged his son. "Hello, Cole. Welcome to our home. Chad is getting you acclimated? Hope you're hungry. It's pizza night, right Betty?"

"Yes. Should be here any minute."

Cole did not get pizza very often. When they did, it was a cheap frozen one with imitation cheese. He only remembered getting a delivered pizza once when they were in Crane. This was going to be a treat.

"Hope you like pepperoni." Chad was excited to make the weekend special for Cole.

"We have a plain cheese pizza too, if you prefer. I wasn't quite sure so I ordered one of each." Betty tried to think of everything.

"*Two* pizzas? Wow." Cole's response confirmed what the Russells already suspected.

Betty remembered what had caused Sam to be late. "Did you get that *favor* worked out?"

"Yes, I received it by courier this afternoon. Mr. Levy took care of his part yesterday and we had it expedited. Cole, it is actually something for you."

"Me? What did my dad do?"

"It was something your mom and dad did. They had a supplemental term life policy for you and your sister in the event of her death. The money has to be put in a trust until you are 18. Your dad gave me permission to form the trust and he said I could advise you on how to invest it. I hope this is not too much, Cole."

Cole already knew that Mr. Russell must be a genius with money. One look around the house convinced him of that. *I would be a fool to say no.* "Thank you, sir, that would be great."

"Excellent! We can talk tomorrow morning before y'all get too worn out by the sun."

"Yes, sir. Can I ask how much?

"Of course. $22000 for you and $22000 for Emily. $6000 was paid out for the funeral."

They all knew that Mike Levy did not spend six grand on that funeral. No flowers and the Navy did all the heavy lifting. Cole didn't care, he was rich. "Can I get a car?"

"Not until you're eighteen, remember."

"Oh, yeah. Well, what should I do with this trust? I don't know what that is really."

The doorbell rang. "Pizza!" Chad screamed as he ran to the door with a stack of fives.

Mr. Russell refrained from getting into details. "We will get into that tomorrow morning. But have you heard of a young computer company called *Apple*?"

Cole shook his head no as they all pivoted toward the pizza. They sat on the screen porch and took in the sun's final descent over the water and into the horizon. The boys stuffed themselves and after their stomach's settled, they hit the pool. They barely made it through the Russell's personal copy of *Footloose* before surrendering for the night.

Cole fell asleep trying to remember everything Mr. Russell had said. *What is Apple?*

After omelets on Saturday morning, Cole accompanied Mr. Russell to the upstairs office. Cole could see the Stono River more prominently now and wished he could be on the blue waters flanked by the lush green foliage. Mr. Russell was accustomed to it, but it was all new to Cole. He stared happily out the window, fantasizing about the boat in the slip. His daydreaming was interrupted as his new mentor began.

"Cole, you are young and you can afford to take some risks with your money. With risk comes great reward. I know you want a car, and we can make that happen for you if that is what you want. I suggest a used one, though. New cars depreciate too fast. This way, you can maximize your contributions to your portfolio."

Cole had no idea what Mr. Russell was talking about. He didn't have any experience here, but long suspected that his dad was hiding money somewhere and his dad had signed off on the whole thing. He realized that twenty-two grand was a lot of money, but not to Mr. Russell.

"I trust you, Mr. Russell. What do you suggest?"

Mr. Russell took time to explain the different strategies and risks associated with each.

"I invest for my clients, and for me. I won't let you put all of your eggs in one basket."

"Last night you mentioned something called *Apple*."

"Yes, I invested heavily when the company went public in '82 and so far I have done well. I haven't sold any of our clients' shares. It is a computer company, and I believe the long-term growth potential could make my clients wealthy. Also, I'm recommending a software company called Microsoft. They own operating systems that are used in DOS-based computers. Walmart is still a good buy."

"I've heard of that one. My mom shopped at the commissary."

"There is more, but I would like to divide it into about twenty of my favorites. I will keep an eye on your trust for you and give you updates. Just don't withdraw until you need it, Cole. That is my advice. You can be a wealthy man one day. I will be careful with your trust and manage it like I would my own. If that is acceptable to you, your dad has already faxed over the documents and the settlement from the life policy will directly fund the trust."

"Sounds good to me. Can I get a car, though?"

"Remember. Get a used one."

"Yes, sir." Cole smiled and said, "Chad and I are going to go fishing now. Is that it?"

"That's it. Y'all go have some fun."

By Monday afternoon, Cole owned shares of stock in Apple, Microsoft, Walmart, Sherwin-Williams, Hasbro, and fifteen safe blue-chip stocks with a history of consistently growing dividends. Mr. Russell continued to update him regularly, and Cole resisted the temptation to cash out. By the time Cole hit forty, his net worth would grow to $4.4 million. But first, he had a life to live.

52

The weekend slipped by quickly. The boys would be committed to their spring football camp now and would not make it back to Chad's house for a few weeks. After classes on Monday, Cole, Chad, and about thirty-five other boys made their way past the cadets in formation, drilling on the quad. The boys were issued lockers and practice gear, but spent the first couple of days in shorts, tees, and their helmets.

Cole was a quick learner. The team walked through the playbook, and Cole soaked it up like a pancake soaked up syrup. He was lean and quick, but mostly, he had grit. Cole wasn't perfect, but like the coaches observed at Foster Creek, Cole learned from his mistakes. When they put on the pads, he went the entire spring without getting squared up for a hard hit.

Chad was competitive, too. As a cornerback, he mainly shined covering the wideouts. He was spared the challenge of trying to cover Cole in the slot. Cole got his bruises learning to block, usually against some bigger-bodied linebacker. The bruises contrasted with his pale skin like India ink spilled onto a white paper towel. The colors ran the gamut from purple to blue before fading to a faint yellow. He didn't care. His ego was getting stroked and it felt good.

By the time camp broke in mid-May, Cole had earned a starting spot for summer camp. As school ended, the boys resumed their weight training and over the summer, Cole put on seven more pounds and grew to nearly six feet tall. Cole would have great memories of that summer. He spent most of it at school or with Chad at the Russell's home.

It was July now, and Cole's teammates were forced into a one-week dead period by the South Carolina Athletic Association. Chad reminded his father of the promise he made to his friends that first night he met Cole. It was the Fourth of July, and Mr. Russell loaded the cooler on the boat, and the boys jumped on board. They carefully navigated their way through the waters that snaked through the marsh until they got to the Stono River, which was already filling up with boats. It would be more dangerous as the day passed, and Mr. Russell was happy to avoid the drunks and headed out to sea.

Three miles off the coast. It was just as Cole had dreamt. The boys fished all day except for a respite from the noon sun when they took refuge under the bimini cover over the deck. They gobbled down the sandwiches and drinks from the cooler and dreamed aloud about their futures. Of course, they would have a boat just like this one. Mr. Russell listened with a wry smile knowing how hard he worked to get it.

Andy wanted to be a professional baseball player. Tegan was going to be an engineer. Chad said he intended to join his father's business after college. Cole had never given it much thought but added that he could see himself as a commercial fisherman.

"Boats are expensive to buy and expensive to keep. Just make sure you have the other stuff paid for first. It can be a money pit."

Mr. Russell had nudged them back into reality, so the boys grabbed their rods and got lost in their own thoughts. The boys caught red snapper and mackerel, and they planned a fish fry during the next week of their vacation. The angled light reflected more brightly off the water now, and Mr. Russell knew that it would be dusk soon. They made their way back to their dock and swapped out the fish for Betty.

Betty Russell was dressed for the occasion. She had a navy sundress with a red, white, and blue scarf and red canvas *Sebagos*. She was ready but for one minor detail. "Y'all stink!"

The boys cackled. Cole had accepted *Y'all* as part of the Southern vocabulary, but he had never heard someone use it that way. Emphasis on the lingering *y'all* followed by a succinct *stink*. But any thoughts of laughing it away quickly disappeared.

"OK boys, quick rinse off in the pool. In and out, we gotta go." The boys took off and jumped in. Sam looked at Betty like he had discovered the wheel.

"You know that's not going to help much."

"Better than nothing though. I will rinse off here." He unwound the hose at the dock and rinsed himself and then hosed down the boat, being careful not to get her seat wet.

"Thank you, Honey. BOYS, OPEN THE CHEST AND GET SOME BEACH TOWELS! LET'S GO Y'ALL!"

The party was in full swing at both Battery Park and the surrounding harbor when *Bonanza* dropped anchor. The cooler had been restocked with assorted soda for the boys and wine for the adults. As the first fireworks filled the sky, Sam and Betty clinked their plastic wine glasses together and kissed. The boys raised their aluminum cans, toasted each other, and mockingly kissed the air around each other's heads. Cole laughed more this day than he had in years. From their vantage point on the southern side of the peninsula, the fireworks rose and seemed to explode over Fort Sumter. Mr. Russell retold the story of the naval battle there. The boys were drawn in and as the final artillery exploded over the water, Cole was at last content.

53

Emily's time with Janet passed calmly as she prepared for her graduation and wedding. She walked across the stage in the gym of Foster Creek to minimal applause from Janet and Billy. Commander McCaster and Cookie always attended the ceremony as most of the graduates every year were linked to the servicemen stationed at the Naval Weapons Station. After the ceremony, they greeted the graduates of the higher-ranking officers that lived behind the gates.

Mike Levy's rank afforded him that right, but he had rejected it to both save a buck and save himself the embarrassment of his wife's social limitations among the other officer's wives. He was still at sea and likely would not have attended even if he wasn't. He had parted with Emily and enough time had passed such that she didn't need him to stir things up again. It was finally over, and she was able to focus on her future. The move to Columbia was only a week away now. The McCasters secured an off-campus apartment with two bedrooms and the lease began June 1. Billy's sister was not thrilled with the idea of Emily as a roommate, but deals were made and she knew she would have it to herself for the spring semester.

"Congratulations, Emily." Billy held her hand as she received congratulatory remarks from people she barely knew.

"It's almost time for us. I'm so excited," Billy spoke softly, leaning in toward her ear.

"Yes. Are you still happy?" It was rhetorical. Encouraged and supported now, she was free to fall deeper for Billy and their baby. The loose threads that bound her to her family were severed. Their love grew with each passing moment. Billy didn't miss a day without seeing her outside of school, but their rendezvous was always at Janet's home. Billy knew his mom's approval was tenuous. Even when he was exhausted from practice, he still went to Emily first.

Plans had been put in place for early graduation for Billy, too. He had already registered for his summer classes and the kids had two weeks to move Emily and marry. Billy's mom had lobbied for an early August wedding partly in hopes that there would not be a baby for some reason. "Things do happen you know," she would argue to Andrew. Billy would have none of it. She was near the end of the first trimester now and she would be showing soon.

The wedding was to be on June 4, 1988, giving the newlyweds a week before Billy returned for his classes. Not an ideal way to start a marriage, but they had a clear path and they were focused on the happy prospects of their future.

The wedding was simple with Billy's parents, sister, and Janet the only guests. She had hoped Cole would come but his anger toward Billy grew when he learned what Billy *is to her.*

Without Mr. Russell to advise her and now eighteen and married, she took the insurance money and bought a car and furnishings for her apartment. She and Billy talked about it and acted before consulting his parents. They would later find they didn't need two cars and by the time they went overseas, Emily's car was sold at a significant loss. The furniture also proved too expensive to ship and was also sold, and by the time they paid the debts incurred by the new baby, she had nothing left. Nevertheless, they were happy.

The only challenges the couple encountered were created by distance. Billy finished his summer classes and had little difficulty with the fall semester. Emily wanted to come to the games but they both realized it would be awkward for the QB's pregnant wife to show up to a high school game. She felt hidden away in Columbia. Nobody even knew Billy was married, but most of his friends felt he had become aloof. He was no longer Billy. Not even to Pete.

Coach Selby noticed it, too. Billy wasn't the only option at QB, but they had entered summer practice thinking he was the best option. At first, the coaches were happy with the new, more mature Billy. But as summer practice ended and they broke camp, the coaches concluded that Billy seemed even more distracted. They wanted their QB to be married to the team. He played just well enough to remain the starter, but the team missed the playoffs and by the end of October, Billy's football career was over.

After every Friday night game, he drove to Columbia. He only missed one weekend during the semester when he took the required ASVAB test for the Navy. His score more than qualified him and he enlisted. In January, he and Emily would ship out to basic training at the Great Lakes Naval Training Center, north of Chicago on Lake Michigan.

54

The grind of the summer finally ended when the BPA Lions broke camp. It was media day in early August. The boys reported to the field eager to see the official results of their summer strength and conditioning program. When Cole stood tall against the wall, he stretched his neck and the tape read 72 inches. He was taller and much stronger now, and he and the other boys went into the season beaming with confidence.

The team won their opener 31 - 14. Alec starred at quarterback, and it was clear to most that the team would struggle if they had to use his backup. Cole caught 3 passes for 47 yards in his first game. One catch was spectacular, but the others were largely due to Alec's accuracy. Cole used his size and quickness to gain at least 20 of his total yards after initial contact.

The optimism waned after the Lions dropped their next two games. Cole had his best game of the year in one of those losses. After falling behind, Alec was forced to throw the ball. Knowing this, the opponent took away any deep strikes and made the Lions settle for short, quick passes. Cole caught nine passes that game for 122 yards and two touchdowns. Yet, he couldn't be happy because the team had lost.

Chad intercepted a ball and returned it for a touchdown in game four and the Lions were back in the win column. Confidence intensified as they won the next three, and they were on the verge of making the playoffs now, standing at 5-2. They needed a win the next week, and they were guaranteed a playoff berth. Instead, they lost against perennial powerhouse Wando High School, and their slim chances vanished as they lost to Myrtle Beach High the following week. The team rallied with a win against Wapoo on Senior Night to finish with a winning record, 6-4. Alec was spectacular, having thrown four touchdowns and amassing 323 yards through the air.

Cole and his teammates learned all the lessons high school boys were supposed to learn playing football. They leaned on each other during times of adversity and celebrated the victories together. They wept with fallen teammates and rallied behind their replacements. The end of a high school football season is a marker for a senior. When the horn sounds, most have played their last competitive game and that reality is, without warning, followed by tears. It is the last time a particular team gets to play together. Next year, every year, is a different team with new players, new strengths, and new chemistry.

It wasn't going to be Alec's last game. He was highly recruited and had narrowed his choice to UNC or Virginia. Still, the comradery Alec formed with this team, *his* team, caused him to be overcome with emotions, too. He was comforted by his parents and then made his way toward Cole.

As Cole observed the interactions with his teammate's parents and their sons on senior night, he couldn't avoid imagining what his senior night would be like. His dad didn't make it to a single game in his junior year. He had the Russells, but they would be comforting Chad. Before he went too far down that road, Alec stood before him, "It's your turn now, Cole. Be a leader."

Cole had the talent, and the boys respected him for his skills. They admired him for his courage with what they knew about his mom and dad. But they still didn't know it all. They would never learn of the real trauma that brought Cole to them in the first place. The weight of a mountain was buried deep within Cole. He could not even consider Alec's suggestion.

"That's a job for someone else."

55

With the first football season at Bishop Porter behind him, the rest of the semester flew by for Cole, and it was his first Christmas break without his mother. He had hoped for a peaceful break, but significant events unfolded that were not in his control.

Cole became an uncle during the Christmas break. Emily gave birth to a son, William Andrew McCaster, Jr. He also spent an uncomfortable few days from Christmas Eve until the day after Christmas with his father at his new apartment in North Charleston. Cole didn't have a room and slept on the couch. There were no reminders of Christmas.

It was the opposite at the McCasters. Everything was decorated there, and Cole appreciated the effort Mrs. McCaster continued to make to keep him distracted and happy. He remembered the presents under the Christmas tree that awaited him upon his return.

His father gave him a twenty dollar bill on Christmas morning and seemed passively interested in his life now. By the time he returned to the Russell home, Cole had learned of a new woman in his dad's life. She arrived on the final morning.

Mike said, "Cole, this is VIcki."

She appeared closer to Cole's age than his father's. The protruding midsection seemed out of place on the otherwise fit and attractive brunette. Cole assumed the ring his dad wore was a tribute to his mom, but he realized it was different now. It matched the ring worn on one of Vicki's claws. Mike Levy had been careless again. He had convinced himself it was love.

"Well Cole, as you can see, you're going to be a big brother."

"No, I am not."

And with that, he was promptly dumped back on the Russell's doorstep. It was the last time that he would speak to his father for many years.

For the next several years, Mike Levy tried to tell himself that Vicki loved him. She was content with the anchor child she bore him until she truly fell in love with a handsome civilian with little money. The child she gave Mike and the baby that provided her safety net were not enough. She had trapped him, too. She left a note explaining it all to Mike Levy.

Mike,

You are a boring old man. No amount of money is worth this. I can see why your last wife drank so much. Take care of Mike Jr. Tell him I died or something when he gets older.

Don't try to find me.

V

One reaps what they sow. Mike Levy was left to raise Junior alone. At first, he tried to be more attentive to Junior than he was to Emily and Cole, but his resentment grew, and he found himself just counting the days until his son would turn eighteen. Junior would come to know about his older brother and sister, but because of their broken relationship with his father, he would speak with them sparingly.

56

Spring football practice flew. Cole hoped the summer of 1989 would mirror that of 1988. But now he spent more time alone on campus rather than at the Russells.

In late May of '89, Mr. Russell attended the funeral of a client. He always cared deeply for the widows and offered to help in any way he could. The widow requested Sam help her get rid of her husband's 'junky old car collection.'

"The cars are taking up the entire basement. The kids don't want them either. I don't care what you get for them. You may have to pay someone to haul some of them off."

As part of the sell-off, Mr. Russell explained to his client about the bad luck that his son's best friend had gone through. He asked if he could acquire one of the cars for Cole. The widow was moved by the story. "I can't sell a car to you for that kid but I'll give one to him. You choose it and surprise him."

Mr. Russell told Cole he got a good deal on the '70 Ford Mustang Shelby. He would explain, "It was just another nearly twenty-year-old antique to the widow. She preferred a new Mercedes, so I got this for next to nothing. If you want it, you can take it now. You probably need to get a little part-time job to pay for your gas and insurance, though."

Cole didn't have to think. "Yes. I want it. Can I pay for it with my trust?"

Mr. Russell told his only lie to Cole. "Yes, I can take care of it tomorrow. You won't even know the money is gone."

That part was not a lie, as the money was never taken from the account.

"Wow. Can I drive it?"

"Well, it's your car. We will need to get insurance first. I'll pay the first premium for you from the trust, but you will need to get a job and pay for the rest."

"Yes, sir," Cole remembered he could not take from the trust until he was eighteen, but he failed to make any connection with the cost of the car or the insurance.

As he drove down the road toward the campus, Cole noticed the *'Help Wanted'* sign in the window of a local coffee shop. He stopped in to talk about the job opening and his newly acquired confidence from the Shelby helped him overcome any insecurity that he would otherwise exhibit. He had the 6:00 AM - 9:00 AM breakfast shift on Wednesday and Thursday because of summer classes and football. On Saturday and Sunday mornings, he worked until the lunch rush began to subside at 2:00 PM. The owner required staff to be efficient and polite, even when customers were rude. They had a steady customer base with lots of regulars that Cole would get used to.

On his first Saturday morning, a manager waved Cole over to take an order from one of the regulars. He approached an average Joe facing away from him reading the Saturday edition of *The Post and Courier*.

He warmly greeted the man, "Good morning sir. Are you ready to order?"

The man recognized something in Cole's gravelly voice. He closed his newspaper and saw the look on Cole's face as he responded, "Cole Levy, I thought I recognized that gruff. Haven't seen you in over a year. How have you been? I was sorry to hear about your mother."

"Hello, Mr. Jaymes." His training would be tested now. *Be polite, especially to the regulars.* "Thank you for that. I am fine now. I go to a private school down the road. I guess you know that. Figured Billy told everybody or something."

"Well, no I didn't know. Billy didn't say much of anything after, you know. Cole, I am sorry about all of that. You know, when I found you…"

"Well, I've moved on from that now. What can I get you?"

Mr. Jaymes was not quite ready to drop it, but he pivoted. "You know, I don't teach anymore. I screwed up too many times, I guess. I should have reported what happened to you the next day, but you told me not to say anything. I've struggled a little with it too, so I can't imagine it was easy for you to forget about it. Another time maybe. How about the breakfast special? Over easy, with bacon and a cheese danish instead of the biscuit, and a glass of chocolate milk."

"Yes, sir. I'll get it right out." Cole could see remorse in Mr. Jaymes, but he felt some vindication knowing that the teacher's small part of his trauma played some role in his dismissal.

Cole delivered the order and checked on Mr. Jaymes periodically while he returned to his newspaper and finished his meal. The diner had become a haven for Mr. Jaymes, and he wasn't going to relinquish his leisurely Saturday and Sunday meals there. Each time Cole stopped by, he fought the temptation to tell more of what he knew.

Over the course of the summer, Mr. Jaymes hinted that he knew more about that night than just his arrival on Sunday morning.

"You know, I tried to warn you about what a snipe hunt meant, but you ran out when the bell rang. I don't know everything, but I can share some things I have heard when you're ready."

"Thank you, but I'm putting it behind me. Are you ready to order? Want your usual?"

"Yes, please."

What Alan Jaymes knew about his nephew, Morgan, and his friend Tom would have to wait.

57

Emily was fighting loneliness as Billy made his way through boot camp then A-School. She was a loving wife and mother, and she was determined not to take the same path as her mom. Billy studied nearly every free moment he had. She knew it was to better their lives, so she supported him in every way. Instead of drawing them apart, it brought them together, and they fell even more deeply in love.

In Virginia, Will was three when he helped welcome his new brother, Davis, to their home. Billy was careful to make sure Will and Davis knew how much he loved them. He was spread thin, but he never wavered from his love for Emily and the kids. He worked hard and studied hard to advance his career.

Just before Will started kindergarten, the family moved to Germany. The McCaster tribe spent the next five years taking advantage of everything Europe had to offer. Billy pampered Emily and the boys. The boys were treated to a life lovingly made for them. They were lucky to not just have to live one. Emily didn't realize at the time that it was these experiences that grounded her. She often found herself feeling guilty for her happiness and the stark contrast of her mother's life with her father's.

Billy and Emily knew they couldn't stay forever. Home was always stateside, and they were beginning to get homesick. Andrew and Cookie had visited more often after Captain McCaster retired. Even Cookie could see how much they loved each other. She had warmed up to Emily. She called often, always checking on what the boys were doing, but sometimes seemingly just to talk with Emily.

It was in early March that they got the orders. Cookie flew over to help Emily purge, sell, and pack for the move. They sold another car for a loss and planned once again to start over with new everything when they arrived in San Diego in June.

58

September 1989

Cole had managed to hurdle many obstacles over the summer of '89. Football and school required him to cut back his hours at the diner. 'Weekends only' was the note on his time sheet that reminded the manager when making out Cole's schedule.

Senior year started fine and Cole and his buddies settled into their routines. Classes were always challenging at the Academy, and it took less than a week before Cole realized he was over his head in calculus.

One day he turned to Chad in class and whispered, "I don't know what a *limit* is but I know I've reached *my* limit."

The whisper was overheard by the cluster around him and the outburst of laughter drew the ire of the teacher. Cole sunk sheepishly into his seat. He stayed in his introverted lane the rest of the semester.

The Lions were only marginally better than the previous season going 7-3 before losing in the first round of the state playoffs. Cole found it difficult to focus. He was distracted by the uncertainty of his future and the haunting of his recent past; memories that seemed triggered by Mr. Jaymes' presence each weekend morning at the diner. It took more of a toll on him than he realized.

The coaches could see something was different. Other more confident boys had passed him by now. The Lion QB was just a placeholder until the sophomore grew into the spot. The team mostly rushed the ball, and Cole often found himself on the bench while the team used an extra tight end for blocking.

Cole also lost his way in other classes, too. Where he was an A/B student his junior year, he didn't make an A his entire senior campaign. His only refuge was random Friday evenings at the Russell home. On Saturday morning, he woke and readied himself for work. By the time he returned in the early afternoon, his demeanor had changed. Chad knew it, but he was too young to know how to help his friend. Behind their bedroom door, Sam and Betty talked about how they could get Cole through this final year.

It was Christmas break again. He had not been contacted by his father, and Cole had accepted the loneliness of abandonment.

The Billy McCaster family was making the trip from Norfolk to Charleston during the holidays and Emily wanted to see her brother. When she told Cole about the visit, he was reluctant and wavered at the prospect of seeing Billy. But he did want to meet his new nephew, so Emily seemed to close the deal when she said, "It's just us now, Cole."

They agreed to meet at a diner in North Charleston. Cole arrived in his blue Shelby to find Emily holding Will. He wasn't expecting Billy. *What the hell!*

Emily read his lips through the windshield, and when he reluctantly opened the door, she reminded him, "It's Christmas, Cole."

His husky voice grunted, and he wanted to get right back in the car, but he stayed nonetheless.

Billy was the first to break the ice. "Cole, this is your nephew Will. Emily thinks he looks a lot like you. I think he looks like her, but I can see it too, since you all have red hair."

Billy took his son from Emily and extended Will toward Cole. Cole acted on instinct and took the toddler. "Can he walk yet?"

"Any day now we think. Just turned one, you know."

"Yes, I remember. I should have brought a present for him, though."

Billy could see Cole spiraling. "Oh no. Meeting you is his present. That is some car you got there. Is it yours?"

"Yes. Mr. Russell found it for me."

Emily chimed in. "Thank God you have them, Cole. They seem to be a blessing from God." The party was on the move.

"They have been. Chad will always be my best friend, too." Cole handed Will back to Billy and was the first to sit.

Billy realized at that moment that any reconciliation with Cole would take longer than Emily hoped. For her, he vowed to be patient. He promised her, and he would not let his wife down. "I hope we can be friends again one day."

"*Again?*" It was rare for Cole to be sarcastic.

"Well, friends one day, then. I do want you to know how sorry I am for the prank. I know it turned into more, but nobody has told us anything. If you ever want to talk about it, I've become a good listener. But let's not do it today. It's Christmas. Right, Will?" He shifted his eyes to his happy toddler sitting patiently in one of the diner's highchairs.

Cole did see a different Billy. He had inklings of it from his weekly visits with Mr. Jaymes. Billy was a Navy man now. He was more like one of his classmates at the academy. More humble, more serious, and perhaps less selfish.

"You know who I see all the time now? Mr. Jaymes."

Billy was surprised. "Does he teach at your school now? He was fired after you left. Did you know that? He wasn't a very good teacher, and I had him in middle school *and* high school. I wasn't very nice to him. I regret that now."

"He is not a very good person either." Cole had accidentally opened the door.

Billy saw the opening, too. "Yeah, I heard some things like that too. You know his uncle was the superintendent or something."

"I didn't know that. And he *still* lost his job? He did tell me he wasn't teaching anymore."

"Yeah, there was something that went on with his nephew that pissed his uncle off. I don't know any of the details though."

"I really don't care either." But Cole did care. He cataloged the conversation and would draw upon it if Mr. Jaymes pushed too hard.

It was time to move on now. Cole was disingenuous when he asked, "How was Chicago?"

"Cold. I would never suggest starting basic in the dead of winter. The city was cool though, but we didn't venture out much with Will being a newborn and all. - School in Texas in the spring and summer was HOT! We wanted Pensacola, but we are more settled now for a longer stay in Virginia. Emily likes it, too. I just got back from my first tour last week. I missed her so much."

They ate as Billy did most of the talking. Cole talked about his football season, and the uncertainty of his future weighing on him.

Billy was the first to utter what everyone else already knew. "Ever consider the Navy?"

59

Cole had turned eighteen in October. He was a man in age but had long since become independent. Still, he could not fully evolve until he graduated high school. He was anxious about his future. The Academy had provided a safety net for him. The Russells had given him the emotional support that he needed to weather the stormy waters of his family dynamic. Having seen Emily so happy, he found himself a little jealous. It just seemed to pile on to the deeply-layered stress he buried inside.

Coach Stoltz wanted the counselor to talk with Cole in the fall, but something always seemed to conflict. Finally, in February, a struggling Cole was summoned to the guidance office.

Cole was invited into a hidden-away office and the counselor took a seat. Introductions were made and once the counselor was comfortable, he proceeded.

"Cole, life is like a sheet in a coloring book. Everybody starts with an outline and has two choices to make. Choice one is how you want to color. Do you want to stay neatly within the boundaries of each object, or do you want to be a little messy? In other words, do you crave organization, or can you handle a little clutter? Some people are a hot mess and their page is like a toddler that just scribbles crayons on the page with no respect to any object."

"I think my mom was that one," Cole offered.

"Well, that could very well be. But you need to discover what kind of coloring makes you happy. Are you staying neatly in the lines and carefully filling each space with color? And then, the colors you pick are the second choice everyone makes. Do you pick a safe life or a bold one? Are you coloring with the primaries, pastels, or maybe neon? Are you adding texture to your objects, depth, and shadows, or are your objects monotone? Everybody has a tolerance for each, and it is difficult when someone tries to pick against their nature. It causes stress in one's life, Cole. Let's talk about your choices as you see them now, and where you see them in the future."

Cole pondered out loud, "Well, I think, I have discovered in being here that I do like structure, and before, I lived with so much drama because everyone around me was coloring outside the lines. I have a need to do everything to the best that I can like when I play football or in my classes, so I guess I fill in the shapes completely."

"I agree Cole, you have great attention to detail. You do exactly what is expected of you."

"Is that a good thing?" Cole was on the verge of a breakthrough, at least for the short term.

"It is neither good nor bad. It is what it is. My perception is that you color nearly within the boundaries, but you don't have any texture yet. As you get older, you will decide how much depth you will give each object in your life. You get to decide what colors you will use, how bold or safe you will play it."

Cole wanted to tell more, but he was coloring out of the eight-crayon box. "I am a lot like my Dad, I think. He is a Navy officer, disciplined and conservative. My sister, Emily, colors over the edges, the objects bleed into each other, and she definitely uses bold colors. For me and Dad, our bananas will always be yellow, but Emily might color hers red or something. We don't talk much anymore since she got married and moved away." Almost as an afterthought, he exclaimed, "And my mom would have just scribbled her entire page black. You wouldn't even see the banana."

Weeks passed and Cole gave a lot of thought about how he was going to live his life, safely or boldly. After careful thought, he weighed his options and decided he was not a risk-taker. *The Navy is the life for me. I look good in blue.*

60

August 2, 1990

It was just Cole's luck. The day he started his basic training, the USA led a coalition into the Persian Gulf to drive Iraq from Kuwait. Cole was athletic and more prepared than most because of the rigorous drills in which he participated at Bishop Porter. He couldn't help but wonder if the training seemed more urgent now that *Desert Shield* was officially underway. He had a brief conversation with Billy as to what to expect. Fall proved a much more tolerable time to complete his training. After basic training, he was sent to his A- school in Meridian, Mississippi. Early December is a difficult month for a Navy family to move, but Cole had no family to speak of; he was excited to get his first assignment. He would ship out to Spain for three years aboard a carrier. First, he had a few calls to make.

"Hey, Chad. It's Cole."

"Dude, I know your voice. How's Navy life?"

"Great. I am going overseas. Mediterranean Sea. That is about all I can say though. How is college life?

"Oh, well you know, harder than what I thought. Very few girls here, but we mix it up with the College of Charleston girls on the weekends. They ignore the freshmen. Everybody calls us *knobs* because of our shaven heads."

"How long does that last?"

"Just the first year. You know who goes to the C of C? Carly Stoltz. I think she is a junior now. Hot as hell!!"

Chad heard the grin in Cole's voice. "You always had the hots for her. As I recall, she didn't want anything to do with you."

"Well, I am a Citadel man now. And you do know that I am *RICH*, right?"

"Uh, no Chad, your dad's rich."

It shook Chad down a little. "True, but one day maybe. But you're getting rich from what I heard."

"Yeah, I guess. I try not to think about it. Talked to your dad last week, and he gave me the update and all. I don't need it yet and it's not that much money. I already have a car."

"Oh yes, how is *Shelby?* Still the love of your life?"

"Actually Chad, that is why I was calling. I have to store her for three years. Your parents have that big basement and I need somebody to drive her every now and then."

"Absolutely. That flashy car is a babe magnet. Probably not for you though." Chad snorted as he laughed. "When?"

"Like, NOW. I will have to have it shipped, so probably by the weekend if that's OK."

"Perfect, just in time for the mixer Saturday night. Carly will melt right into my arms."

Chad heard the gravelly grunt on the other end of the line, "Good grief!"

61

January 1994

To: Chadrussell12@hotmail.com
From: Colelevy1@hotmail.com

"What's up Chad? Cole here. Thought I would try my hand at this email thing you told me about. Well, lots to talk about, so here it is. I am being shipped back to stateside, probably Norfolk, Virginia. I re-enlisted and got a nice bump. Talked to your dad the other day and sent the bonus to my account. Need to get *Shelby* back. Sorry. Hope everything is going well. Your dad said you and Carly are pretty serious now. Wow, I can't believe it, Must've been my car. Haha. Well, we will talk soon buddy."

To: Colelevy1@hotmail.com
From: Chadrussell12@hotmail.com

"First of all, genius, you don't have to say 'It's Cole' when I can clearly see it is from COLELEVY1. Haha. Secondly, your timing is perfect. I was going to call you with some news anyway, but it is hard to connect with you over so many time zones. Glad you joined the 20th century. Well, I am getting married. Yep, I swept Carly off her feet and she succumbed to my charm. *Shelby* only helped me get over the first hurdle. You know, I have a new BMW now. New to me anyway. Dad said I need to look like I am successful so he helped me get it. Did he tell you I am joining his firm after I graduate? Maybe he will give me your account. Haha. Well, let me just say it. There is only one choice for my best man. Can you get leave for that? Will you be out to sea or do you know? We are looking at the first weekend in June. Andy, Tegan, and a few guys from here will be groomsmen. Mom is helping with the wedding. Coach Stoltz is lost. Haha.

How is your love life? You remember Carly's sister, right? Haha????"

To: Chadrussell12@hotmail.com
From: Colelevy1@hotmail.com

"Yes, I remember Sarah, but I also remember what you had said about her. Haha. Sounds like too much for me. Nobody serious right now. The Navy uniform is the real magnet though. The girls always want a 'relationship' though, and I ain't ready for that yet. Anyway...

First, NO WAY IN HELL do you get my account. I would have to finally pull it out first. Haha. Second, of course, I will be your best man. I should have no problem in June, but I will double-check and let you know if the Navy has a problem with the date."

62

There was something about seeing Chad's happiness that pushed Cole to reach out to his sister. He wanted what Chad had. To get it, he would have to bet his secrets.

To: Billysgirl88@AOL.com
From: Colelevy1@hotmail.com

"Well, this is hard to say. I need to talk to Billy next time you are both stateside. I keep thinking back about what happened before Mom died, and it is keeping me from living my best life. I think this is an in-person thing, not a phone or email thing. I will fly to meet you both if I need to. I am in Virginia."

It was late at night when Cole finally hit the send button. He knew Emily was just getting up in Germany. Surely she would see the email soon, and he hoped she would send an email the next day. He didn't want to dwell on it, but he had a long history of internalizing everything. This night would be no different.

Cole tossed and turned until 1:00 AM when he was awakened by the light of his phone. He flipped it open, swallowed around the knots in his throat, and hit the answer button.

"Well, that didn't take long."

Emily was to the point. Finally, Cole was ready to talk to her, and she didn't want to risk him changing his mind.

"Of course not, Cole. You had to know I would call as soon as I saw your email. Sorry about waking you up, but I wanted to call before the boys got up. It's summer break here so they sleep until around 8:00. What time is it there?"

"It's oh one hundred. I wasn't asleep though. How is everybody?"

"Wonderful. We went to Bruges last weekend. It's the 'Venice of the North.' Loved the quaint shops on the canals. The kids loved the chocolates. Billy is great. He left about an hour ago. In three weeks he leaves on a six-month tour. We are coming to Charleston next week for six days of leave. Is that too soon to meet?"

Cole began to question what he had started. He was ready, but this was fast. Still, he was eager to meet before he lost his nerve.

"I'll try to catch a flight. I am off Wednesday. Will that work?"

"We will make it work. Want to meet at the same place as last time?"

"Yes, but you might want to leave the kids with the grandparents this time," Cole suggested.

"Absolutely. I love you, Cole, and I am proud of you."

"I love you, too, Emily. I'll email you to confirm, and we can set the time. See you soon. Bye."

When he flipped the phone shut, Cole took a deep breath and when he exhaled, he felt the weight of years of anxiety begin to leave his body. He closed his eyes and fell asleep on a boat in the Caribbean, fishing with Chad and the boys.

63

Cole was able to catch a flight to Charleston on Wednesday and arrived an hour after take-off. He didn't have any checked bags or carry-ons, so it was straight out the door where he saw Emily in a rented minivan. The last time Cole and Emily had ridden together in a minivan was with their mother, but neither recognized the irony. They were together, in fact, to discuss events that indirectly contributed to her death.

Cole asked about the boys. Billy proudly told of Will's peewee soccer heroics in Germany and Davis's progress in potty training. Emily talked about upcoming trips through Europe. She talked about what life was like there. Before she could say more than Cole wanted to hear, Billy was parking the van at the familiar diner in North Charleston.

Billy knew Cole would talk when he was ready. This was Cole's meeting, he would give him space, but someone had to start the ball rolling.

"I can't remember what I got last time. Must not have been good then. What are you thinking about ordering Cole?"

On this day, Cole's voice sounded like he had gargled with a cup of sand. His thin lips were more evident now that the emphasis was off the gap in his teeth. Two teeth were late bloomers and acted like an angry mob pushing his front teeth together. Cole rarely smiled, but now he had the smile of a millionaire. He was more confident, and he was resolved to get this day over with.

"I think I had the meatloaf, but I don't remember. I have to fly back in a few hours, so I don't want to eat heavy. Still, it is meatloaf."

The waitress came and took the orders. After the drinks came, Cole shifted a few times and then settled into his chair. He had rehearsed it a thousand times, but now he had forgotten the script.

"Well, I don't know how to start. I guess I just came to the realization that I can't continue to let this eat away at me. The only way to move forward is to stop thinking back. Billy, I hope you will understand more about why I am still so angry after I tell you everything. Emily, don't overreact."

Billy looked empathetic and could see how difficult this was for Cole. Too many words would be risky. Cole could still shut it all down. He and Emily needed some closure, too. "Take your time."

"Well, I stayed out there until around 11:00, then I started home..."

Cole swallowed another cup of sand and the first words finally leaked out as he told all he knew.

64

Saturday, March 28, 1988

As Billy drove away, Pete quickly recognized the approaching lights were not of his mom's car. Two boys drove up in an old Olds with a loud muffler. "Hey, Pete. What are you doing out here?"

Pete went to the same church with Tom Riddick before Tom's family moved to Moncks Corner. He was two grades ahead but at the time, they were part of the same middle school group at church.

"Waiting on my mom. What are y'all doing *here?*" Pete knew the other boy, too, It was Morgan Jaymes, senior QB at Berkley High. The county wasn't that big. He saw the toilet paper and a can of spray paint in the backseat. "What are y'all going to do with that?"

Morgan was almost dismissive but decided to spill the plan. "Going to pull a little prank on you guys. Just in fun, ya' know? You like pranks, right?"

Pete was quick to gain their approval. "Oh yeah. Me and Billy played a big prank on one of our friends tonight. It was EPIC."

Morgan laughed. "I bet."

"No, really."

"What did you do then?" said Tom.

Eager to impress the older boys, Pete described the plan Billy drew up. To seal the deal he added, "Billy's probably screwing his sister right now. Kid is still out there waiting for a snipe too."

Wheels were turning in Morgan's mind. "Hey man, we got some liquor. Take a sip."

Pete turned up the bottle and felt the burn in his throat. Tom laughed and he said, "Get in Pete, we'll take you home." Pete opened the rear door and jumped in the backseat.

The car turned right out of the school parking lot. After 100 yards, Pete turned around and saw his mother's headlights turn into the school. "I live the other way."

"Don't be a pussy, Pete."

"I'm not. Give me another swig."

Just before eleven, Morgan delivered Pete to the front of his driveway, U-turned, and drove away. As they saw Foster Creek High lit in the full moon, Morgan turned to Tom and said, "Wonder if that kid is still out there?"

"Are you thinking what I'm thinking?" Tom looked at Morgan and nodded his head in the affirmative. The car turned into the lot, and they drove around toward the side of the school so the car could not be seen.

Cole heard a muscle car in the distance as he stood and picked up the blue snipe bag. He left the marshy area having bagged ZERO snipe and made his way through a blue moonlit path through the pines back toward the school. He could see the football stadium through the trees on his right, and he knew the school was straight ahead. As he reached the edge of the woods, he felt a forceful thump as his back was slammed against a tree. He dropped the snipe bag and before he could recover it, two stronger people grabbed his hands and pulled them behind the tree. He heard the sound of the loosening adhesive before he felt it tightly around his hands. He turned to look, only to find one of the boys placing the bag over his head. He heard the buttons on his flannel shirt hit the ground.

"What are you doing?" Now bound to the tree, Cole had little chance. His quiet nature would fail him now as he couldn't say more.

"Shut up or I'll gut you." Cole could smell the alcohol on them and did not yet know their intent. Morgan Jaymes' intent was just to have a little fun, and then let him go, but the situation escalated quickly. Cole kicked at the air. A man caught a foot and slammed it against the tree. Morgan's friend then pulled his jeans down to his ankles.

"Tom, tape his feet next." Morgan almost snickered aloud.

Cole had a name now. He heard the tape loosen from the roll again. Simultaneously, he found his ankles loosely bound together. His shoes made a thump as they hit a tree nearby.

Tom looked toward Morgan, "Did you bring the bottle? Let's give him a drink."

Cole heard the other man jogging away. Time had no meaning now. As the sounds of the footsteps faded away, he felt Tom's hands yanking his boxers to his taped ankles. He heard a rattling sound next, but he could not connect the sound to the object. His fading focus on the sound was quickly replaced as he heard the can hit the ground and felt Tom's hands move lightly up his thighs.

"Don't do that!" Cole yelled. He thought the worst and although his range was limited, he moved the man's target as best he could. His chest worked hard to get enough air to push out the words, "Please, stop."

Cole felt the hot breath before the man was on him. When Tom heard the car door slam in the distance, he finally pulled his head off of Cole just before they heard Morgan's footsteps as he appeared from around the building. Cole heard a click and then felt a cold steel blade on his scrotum. He tried not to think about it. The rattle returned. He heard the hiss and then felt the cold wet air where the boy and blade had been. The sounds of the footsteps suddenly stopped. Even though he didn't see it, Morgan knew that Cole had been sodomized by Tom. He then saw Tom emptying the can of blue paint onto Cole's genitals.

"Come on, let's go," Morgan demanded.

Tom lingered for a moment and then Cole felt the spray of more paint over his waist and arcing over his thighs; one last violation of his body. He heard the cap click on the can. His captor leaned in and whispered, "Tell anybody about this, and I'll turn you from a bull into a blind steer."

After what Tom had done over the past several minutes, Cole believed every word. Cole felt a few wet drops of blood trickle down the inside of his leg. He heard the footsteps disappear around the building and he was wary of their return. *What next?* He soon heard two car doors shut in unison. The engine rolled over, and Cole sighed as they drove away. It was the kind of sigh that a man makes when he knows the worst is over, but too much is still unknown. He was alone now and terrorized. He tried to loosen his hands. Thirty minutes later, he caught his only break. The seam on the bag got snagged on the bark and he thrust his head forward enough to open the noose. He squatted just enough to remove his head before the bag fell back into his hair. He shook it off; it fell to the ground. He could see his pale skin now in the bright moonlight. He saw he was naked and he confirmed what he thought. He was generally painted blue from his waist to his mid-thighs.

It took what felt like hours for Cole to shuffle his mindset. He was a victim, but he needed to survive it. He tried to imagine how it would end but couldn't stop reliving it. By the time the moonlight sank behind the school, it was nearly daylight, and he sank to the ground. Time passed quickly and he dozed off and on. The sun broke the horizon, and he was strengthened by the light of the day. After screaming for help for nearly two hours, he saw the first arrival for church.

65

January 1994

Billy sat motionless as Cole finished.

"Did Mom know any of this?" Emily lifted the flimsy paper napkin beside the plate and wiped away the tears. Billy pulled her tightly toward him to comfort her, but his focus was still on Cole.

"Yeah, she found out at school. Mr. Jaymes told the principal about how he found me. She knew I had been tied up but that's it, I think. Mom was the one that called Bishop Porter. That changed my life. I resented it at first but it turned out to be one of the only good things she ever did for me. You know, I wasn't going back to Foster Creek because of Mr. Jaymes. I couldn't face him or ya'll. Too embarrassed I guess."

"That makes sense now. I never could understand how a simple snipe hunt would cause you to miss a week of school, much less transfer elsewhere. I know we weren't friends then, but I really wasn't friends with anyone. I don't think anybody liked me. I wouldn't like me either back then. I was a smart ass. I will say, though, that as I fell more for your sister, I had hoped I would become friends with you, too. I made an error in judgment. Blinded by love, I guess."

Cole could tell that Billy had bottled up guilt, and he needed to release it. There was a lot to untangle and little time left to do it. Cole was not selfish, and he wanted to give Billy and Emily the time they needed to digest what he fed them. But first, Cole needed to address Emily about their mother before Billy could have some closure.

"I feel like mom was distracted. I know it was an accident, but I can't understand why she was out near the Station that day. She had just dropped me off earlier that day, and I saw she was upset when she left. She didn't know enough about what happened. It was like she was hiding something."

Emily nodded in agreement. "She was unhinged when she returned. I didn't know where she had been, and I didn't know anything about your whereabouts. If I had known, I wouldn't have told her about Billy and me, or about being pregnant. She shut it down after I told her that. I think she was on the way to see Billy's mom when the accident happened. You know that she was unhappy with Dad and everything else. There were rumors about some other stuff, too, but I didn't want to know. Janet tried to tell me some things, but I just didn't take the bait."

"Yeah, nothing would surprise me. Do you hear from Dad?"

Emily's eyes bulged. "Uh, he will never talk to me again. He resented me. You know the only reason he married Mom was because of me, right? He never treated me like he did you."

"Because of you? You mean she was pregnant with you?" Cole seemed surprised but it reconciled some things that he never understood. "Well, are things better with your family, Billy?"

Billy and Emily both recognized that Cookie McCaster was making more of an effort now. Billy gave a quick progress report. "She is not as angry, and she loves the boys so much. After Davis was born, I think she realized it was all for real. She is beginning to see Emily the way I do now."

Emily chimed in, "Yes, definitely not as awkward."

"You mentioned Mr. Jaymes earlier and I want to circle back to that a second. I heard that he was fired because of something that happened with his nephew. Pete knows something about it, but he stopped short of telling what it was. I wish we could talk to Mr. Jaymes to find out if there is some connection. But I don't have any idea how to go about that."

Cole gave it some thought. He had come this far, why not complete the journey? He told Billy of the uncomfortable encounters he had with Mr. Jaymes at the diner during his senior year. He recalled that Mr. Jaymes seemed to want to give away some secrets about that night, too. It was coming together now.

"I know where he is every weekend morning, but I've got to fly back this afternoon."

Billy agreed to confront Mr. Jaymes and get to the bottom of it. He got the name of the diner and made plans with Emily to confront him. They were on the same team again now. But it was a one-game season, and they were down to the final plays.

"I have to find Pete."

66

Billy enlisted his dad's help and after a day of investigation, they had the mobile number for Pete. Billy extended the antenna on his new Nokia 6110 phone and dialed the number. Mr. McCaster gave him a funny look and then said, "We have a phone, you know." He had wanted to know the reason for finding Pete and hoped to know more from the phone call. Billy wanted privacy though and opted to move with his new toy to the outside porch.

"Pete, you're a hard man to track down. Do you know who this is?"

Pete sounded as dense as always. "No, who is this and how did you get my number? It's unlisted."

"It's Billy. Billy McCaster. Do you remember me from high school?"

"Oh, Billy. Yes, I remember." Pete remembered how Billy just stopped being his friend after the night of the snipe hunt. He remembered that they were on the verge of getting suspended. Mostly, he remembered what happened that night that did *not* include Billy. As he remembered, he became nervous.

"What do you want?"

Billy recognized the tension in Pete's voice. He decided to apologize first and offer the reason why he couldn't be the Billy he knew after that night.

"So you married Emily Levy? And you have two kids."

"Yep, happy as a lark. What are you doing now?" Billy knew there was a time when Pete would walk on water for him. He also knew that this was not the current state of their relationship.

"I am a welder here in Biloxi. I work in the shipyards. I ain't married or nothing. I have a girlfriend, though. She works as a waitress at a nearby casino. I met her while me and some buddies were playing blackjack. I am thinking about asking her to marry me."

"That sounds great, man." *That souns horrible man.* "You sound happy. I'm happy, too, but I'm calling because of Cole. Do you remember Emily's brother, Cole?"

Pete wanted to play dumb but the awkward silence already told Billy that Pete indeed remembered Cole. "Yes. I haven't seen him since, you know…"

"Right. Well, I am trying to help Cole because he has been unhappy for a while now. He told me about some boys that did some horrible things to him that night after we left. He seems to think Mr. Jaymes knows something that will help, but I wanted to ask if you can tell me about what happened to you before you got home that night."

Pete unloaded his secrets on Billy. He told of how Morgan and Tom literally kidnapped him. Most importantly, he told of how Morgan bragged about how his uncle had gotten them liquor.

Billy wondered if these were the same boys that tormented Cole. The timeline seemed to fit. The alarm sounded as Pete added, "One last thing Billy. I told them about the joke we were playing on Cole."

67

Cole had told his brother-in-law the most likely time to catch Mr. Jaymes at the diner was 8:30 AM. Emily and Billy pulled in around 8:15 and after Billy checked out the customers, he returned to the minivan and they waited. Around 8:35, Billy saw Alan Jaymes enter the diner alone, just as Cole had predicted. They decided to give him time to order and get served before they casually ran across him. It would be after some reminiscing that Billy would turn the conversation into more of an investigation.

"Mr. Jaymes? It's Billy, Billy McCaster. From Foster Creek High School?"

"Yes, I remember you, Billy. How have you been?"

Billy could already tell that this was a different Mr. Jaymes. *Why did I expect differently? I am not the same.* He decided to take a more direct approach.

"Well, to be honest, Cole told me I could find you here. I am trying to help Cole work through some things, and I think you can help."

Billy didn't have to work very hard, Alan Jaymes was eager to help. "I've been wanting to help Cole for years, but he just seemed to be disinterested in anything that I had to say. I told him I wanted to tell him some things when he was ready. I need to tell him directly though. What I know could be embarrassing, and I won't risk hurting him by telling someone else. I learned from that night, too. I hope you understand Billy."

"Certainly. I am relieved to hear some of this. This is my wife, Emily.

Emily is Cole's sister. I can tell you that Cole has told us everything that happened to him that night and the next morning, including the way you found him. I don't know how much *you* know either so suffice it to say, we both need to tread carefully. I talked to Pete, and he said he met two boys that night in a late-model red Olds Cutlass with a hole in the muffler. He told them about Cole and we think they went back and..."

Mr. Jaymes interrupted, "...did some horrible things to him. Sounds like we both know the sordid details. Yes, I know who they are and that is what I wanted to tell Cole years ago. One of the boys is my nephew, Morgan. I bought him liquor that night. I've lost a lot of sleep since he finally told me what they did to Cole. He was with a kid named Tom, and he said he had no idea that Tom would take it to another level. When he saw what Tom was doing, he made him leave. I asked him why he didn't go back and untie Cole. He said he was afraid of going to jail.

I made terrible mistakes leading up to that night, too. I tried to warn Cole about what a snipe hunt meant. I bought liquor for my nephew. Mostly, I didn't report the way I found Cole, but that was only because he told me not to. I thought you and Pete tied him up until my nephew told me the whole story a couple of years later. I wanted to see if Cole needed to pursue things legally with the boys, ya know? He was so adamant about not telling anyone, I still didn't want to break his trust."

It was not what Billy expected. Alan Jaymes was contrite. He was genuine and the events had affected him, too. "I need to tell Cole all of this. Where can we find Tom and your nephew, Morgan?"

"Ironically, Morgan *is* in prison. Alcohol turned to drugs and drugs led to dealing. He was always a dumbass. Tom died in a car accident the summer after he graduated. I think that is what led Morgan down a dark path, too."

"I see. How long will Morgan be in prison?"

"I have no idea. He had a DUI and a drug possession charge before he was busted for dealing. He's in a federal prison so probably for a very long time. I don't even know which prison. I haven't spoken to that part of my family since I read about it in the papers."

Billy and Emily knew this would likely be enough. Tom had died and Morgan was in prison. "I think this is good enough."

"I am glad to finally get it off my chest. I was hoping I could ask Cole for his forgiveness after I told him. Please tell him I am sorry for my part."

Emily said, "You couldn't have known what would have happened."

"Thank you for that."

68

On Saturday afternoon, Billy picked up the landline and phoned Cole. He told him about his conversation with Pete and then about meeting Mr. Jaymes. He detailed what he learned about Morgan and Tom. Billy tried to convey Mr. Jaymes's temperament and remorse but in actuality, Billy was still too young to interpret Mr. Jaymes' thoughts properly. Cole had to rely on his recall of the last conversations from the summer at the diner. Between the two of them, they managed to appreciate the difficulty Mr. Jaymes encountered.

Cole's emotions were not a light switch. He had hoped that after he learned about the why's and the who's he could just flip a page and be done with it. Information is power and rather than turning a page in the book he was living, Cole learned that he was able to write a new book now. The information Billy gave him and the closure he had from Tom's death eventually allowed him to begin to heal. Cole could never forget it, but as time passed it impacted his thoughts and actions less. When he did think about it, he always hoped that it would be the last time. He and Billy were on speaking terms now. They spoke often but the conversations about the snipe hunt were never revisited.

69

April 2000

"Hello, this is Cole."

Chad laughed. "How many times do I have to tell you? I know it's you 'cause I called your number."

"I don't know, habit I guess. What's up, buddy?"

"I am here with Dad and we wanted to give you an update and all. Do you have a few minutes?"

"Of course."

"Well, are you keeping up with your account online?"

"Now and then I will look at it, but I don't look at the details. I can't believe I have that much money now."

"Believe it, dude! $221,000. Did you see that we traded out of Hasbro and bought a position in this new online bookseller?"

"Yes, I trust you, but I don't know how a bookstore can be a great investment."

Mr. Russell chimed in. "*Amazon* has long-range plans to be more than a bookstore. Think *Walmart* of the internet. And I am doubling down on *Apple*. I have reinvested most of your dividends from other stocks to buy more shares."

"I was wondering how I owned so many shares now. You told me about the stock split before. I don't need any of it so I guess I will let it ride."

"Yes, a client asked me how long I should hold a stock like that. My response was 'forever.'"

Cole was almost bored with the talk of money. "Hey Chad, when are you and Carly going to give your parents a grandchild?"

Sam Russell chuckled. "Yes, Chad, when is that going to happen?"

Chad grinned at his dad, "Well, funny that you asked. And the bigger news, as you know twins run in Carly's family. So, Dad, I am going to need a raise."

70

May 2000

"Hey, Sis. This is Cole. Sorry I missed you. Hope you and the boys are doing well. I am getting settled in my new apartment. I forgot how beautiful San Diego is. Call me on my cell when you get a chance." After an awkward pause, Cole's raspy voice managed "I think I can be happy here...Bye."

Cole had just re-enlisted and after 10 years in the Navy, he finally got his first choice for a base assignment. He remembered times of his childhood when life was more innocent. Choosing between Crane and San Diego was a no-brainer. With the reenlistment, Cole received the customary signing bonus. He still had most of his other bonuses in savings. He already had a car and was not yet ready for a house. Subconsciously, he followed the blueprint that his father designed years ago. Being near the blue waters of the Pacific was spiritual for Cole. He lost himself when he fished from the dock of his apartment complex, admiring the boats in the harbor from afar. He would have long periods of peace, but Cole's demons occasionally gnawed at him like a hound on a T-bone, failing to be deterred until he was fully consumed. Cole was determined to overcome it.

His phone rang. He reached with his right hand into the right pocket of his jeans and pulled out his cell, flipped it open, and said, "Hello."

Emily said, "Are you OK? You sound tired."

He recognized her voice and the demons left him alone. "Emily!!! How are you? I tried to call earlier to see how it's going."

"I got your message and everything is great." She knew she still had to carry the conversation along. "Germany is cold and the culture here is so different. It is everywhere in Europe." She covered the phone and turned toward Will. "It's my brother, Cole, in California. I'll be done in a little while. Let me talk now...OK, I will."

"Cole, sorry 'bout that. Will and Davis say hi."

"How are they?"

"Adjusting like the rest of us. Will is literally shivering right now. Germany is COLD. He refuses to wear enough layers. You know all about that."

"What? Huh?"

"You remember when Mom would chastise you in Crane when..."

"Yeah, yeah. I remember now." They shared a laugh.

"So, San Diego. And you signed up for how many more years?"

"Just two this time. I am mostly through college now. Gonna finish before I leave though."

"Mom would have wanted that Cole. Billy says hi, too. He is out the door now. Sorry."

Awkward silence. Finally, she said, "I have some news for you too. You will never guess where we are being deployed to."

"Are you kidding? San Diego?"

"Yes. We will be there next month. Billy and the boys can't wait to go fishing with you."

With that, the conversation was rejoined by other voices in Cole's head. He was not sure if he was quite ready to share his life, but the choice was not completely his. He congratulated them and promised to help, but Cole was ready to go.

"Well, I'm outside fishing, and it looks like rain so I better get everything back in the apartment. I'll call you when I get more settled. I love *YOU*. Tell Will to button up, OK? Guess I will see you soon. Bye."

"OK. Bye, Cole."

Emily wished she and Cole could be closer. She wished that Cole could at least say that he loved Will and Davis, too. She wished she could lay in a tri-fold vinyl lounger on a pontoon boat and watch Cole teach her boys how to fish. Cole and Billy, together, fishing with Will and Davis.

He remembered his father's promise of a boat in Charleston. He remembered why it never happened. He felt abandoned by his dad, but he had a few fond memories of fishing off the pontoon with his Dad in Crane.

Instead of sending his bonus to his account with Mr. Russell, Cole added some of his personal savings and altered the blueprint of his life. His new boat was a 2000 *Wellcraft 270 Coastal*. It had a box for the fish and could navigate both harbor and the sea. At first, he trailered the boat, but it required at least 2 people just to get it in the water. He soon realized that he was spending too much time picking up the boat, driving to the water, putting in, taking out, dropping the boat back off to storage, and driving back to his apartment. Besides, he just wanted to be alone and didn't enjoy fake conversations with a buddy he would never learn to trust. Chad remained his best friend, and they talked often but he had seldom seen him since the wedding.

Soon, Cole rented a boat slip at a nearby marina. On days off, he would arrive at his cruiser in the afternoon and sleep on the boat. Below board, the cabin had a v-berth forward, a small kitchen mid, and a small shower area with a toilet aft. The boat was both a confidence booster for Cole and an aphrodisiac for the women of the area looking to hook up with any Navy man with a bar on their uniform. It was not fishing for Cole. It was more like catching. The boat and his uniform were all the bait he needed. Girls were plentiful in San Diego. Cole fished for sport but the ladies were using different bait. They were trying to land the big one, a Navy officer.

When he needed sex, all that was required was a cliche. "Can I buy you a drink?" Women melted when he spoke, finding his raspy voice nearly irresistible. Half an hour later they were pulling away from the marina. Cole had an All-American look, boyish charm, and he was good at sex. Cole was good at everything. Good, not great. He was both perfectly imperfect and simplistically complicated. Girls were easily hooked, but Cole was a 'catch and release' guy. He was not an asshole; he just had issues. He was a man and if not for his primal desire to plant his seed, he would not even bother. But Cole didn't like to garden, and he was not a risk-taker. His seeds were always protected. He could always tell when one of the ladies was trying too hard, "You don't have to use that."

His hoarse voice always firmly responded, "Yes, I do." He remembered what his sister told him about his mother, and how she lured his father that way.

It was not the companionship that he wanted and he usually felt a little guilty. Afterward, a courtesy cuddle and then back on deck. He might fish a little before insisting that he take his lady back to shore. Soon, he was empty and alone again and his thoughts would start to betray him.

The Navy had taught Cole discipline. He was smart and highly educated. He was conservative with his money, just as he was taught by his father and reinforced by Mr. Russell. He still sent 10% of his monthly check to Mr. Russell for an IRA and to add to his trust. He colored the spaces in his life as he was expected, but rarely added the rich texture that was needed to make him truly happy. Perhaps he needed a wife, but the only happy marriage he had ever seen was that of Chad's parents. Except for the boat, Cole was playing it safe. He colored the shapes carefully, but just to the edge. He fought his depression and kept it to himself. He would not surrender to it. His mother had. He vowed to be better. His page would not be black scribbles. His life was neatly colored, but only in shades of blue.

The McCasters made it to San Diego as promised. With family close, Cole and Emily Levy were able to bolster the knots of the threads that had begun to bind them together again.

On a sun-drenched Sunday afternoon. Cole fueled the tank at the dock, and Emily and Billy loaded the coolers and placed the life jackets on Will and Davis. The sky was a rich, powder blue. As the land disappeared from view, the ocean changed to an endless deep shade of marine blue. The dull tones that dominated Cole's thoughts were no longer with him on this outing. He felt love and friendship now. He looked at Billy struggling to help the boys cast the lines. Cole thought of Chad and his father. He thought of the fishing trips on the Russell boat. He was filling up on fond memories now. Cole saw Billy's desperation and plea for help.

"I got this, Billy."

As Cole instructed the boys, warm colors flooded his soul.

71

February 2003

Emily and Billy had been on a mission to find a wife for Cole. After countless attempts, they had all but given up. Chad and Carly visited often. Carly's sister, Sarah, was in LA now and they devised a plan to bring her along next time they met Cole.

> To: Colelevy1023@gmail.com
> From: Chadrussell1214@gmail.com

"Hey, buddy. We are coming out west again next month. Are you going to be in town this time? We missed you last time. Hope you are back from your cruise now. The twins are great but we need a little break. Planning around your schedule this time so let me know."

> To: Chadrussell1214@gmail.com
> From: Colelevy1023@gmail.com

"Hey, It's Cole. I just got back last week. I got another promotion to First Class Petty Officer, so you can help me celebrate. Talked to your dad last week about how to shelter some of this money. Interesting job you guys have. I am on my way out to see Will play in a soccer game. He is so much better than the other boys on the middle school team. Hope you can meet them all one day."

A plan was hatched. When Chad and Carly arrived at LAX, Sarah was there waiting for them. Sarah was not like Carly. They were fraternal twins, Sarah was a natural brunette, but their hair was colored in nearly identical tones. Sarah had bought into the west coast lifestyle. A month ago, she had confided in Carly that she was in between boyfriends again.

"Do you have plans tonight? We are starving," Carly delivered her rehearsed line.

"No. No plans. I know a quaint little place to get some dinner. Very fresh local food prepared with an Asian twist. It is one of my favorites. Is that cool?" It was a rhetorical question. Sarah always had control over Carly and they both knew it.

Chad chimed in, "Sounds great."

As they walked toward the baggage claim, Chad looked ahead and acted surprised as he said, "Hey, that's Cole."

"Hey Buddy, what are you doing here?"

Cole and Sarah were not stupid. Sarah remembered Cole from Bishop Porter, but this was a man standing before her now. A confident and handsome man. She decided to see it play out.

"Well, you did ask me to pick you up here," Cole said with a hint of skepticism about Chad's ploy. Chad had talked Sarah up for years. Cole was able to put those conversations behind him as Sarah was more attractive than he remembered. *What are you cooking up?*

Chad's rehearsed lines did not hit the mark. "We must have messed up. We talked about asking each of you, so I guess we got our signals crossed. Right Carly?"

"Uh, Hum." Carly, Cole, and Sarah said in unison.

Carly delivered her next line. "Well, we are all here now, and we were going to get some dinner. Sarah knows this fabulous place. Cole, can you please join us?"

Sarah smiled at Cole, "Yes, Cole, can you *please* join us on this unplanned dinner?"

Cole was taken by her smile and her wit and responded in kind, "Oh, yes. I wouldn't miss seeing Chad and Carly squirm for all the tea in China."

"Good Grief. Ok then, Who has a car,?" Chad responded.

"We both do. You didn't think of that did you?" Sarah taunted them and Cole laughed.

"I'll ride with my sister and Cole can catch up with Chad. Chad, follow us."

Sarah questioned Carly for the forty-minute ride to the restaurant. It was not about the plan as much as it was about Cole. She was interested. He looked striking in his Navy whites. She asked about his experience with dating and was happy to learn that he was and forever had been unattached.

Chad talked Sarah up as they followed the girls. Cole was used to it from Chad, but putting a face to the name again piqued his interest.

"So she lives in LA now?" Cole was nibbling on Chad's line.

"Yes. Pretty sure I have told you this. She works in advertising for a studio. I told you she was beautiful, right? She is successful too. And she is single."

"Slow down, Chad. It's just dinner. You are trying too hard now. Yes, she is attractive, but I see lots of pretty women, you know."

Chad thought for a moment. He had gotten this far and didn't want to misstep. "You're right. Let's just have dinner and see how it goes. Nobody is planning a wedding or anything."

"Well, you seemed to have gone through a lot of trouble to plan this so it wouldn't surprise me if you already had,"

Chad was squirming, so he was relieved that they had arrived at the restaurant.

As they made their way inside, Cole opened the door for Sarah. "What do they have here?"

"It's Asian fusion cuisine. Lots of fresh fruit and local vegetables. I hope you like it." Sarah realized that it sounded like she was more interested in Cole than Chad and Carly. "I hope you all like it."

It did not escape Cole what had just happened. "Well, it sounds delicious. There is a place like this in San Diego that I like. I'll give it a review after we eat, and we can compare notes."

The restaurant had an open-air courtyard where patrons sat under a market umbrella and enjoyed the California climate. It was early evening, and the sun was lower in the sky. The weathered brick was covered with flowering vines that masked the bleaching of the sun. Tall, exotic plants cast filtered shadows over the courtyard. The tables were arranged to take advantage of a large fireplace that kept the customers warm and cozy. Sarah had not realized how romantic the place was as she had only dined there with friends. She was slightly embarrassed that she did not make the connection before it was too late.

Chad was unwilling to let things move along naturally. He didn't trust Cole with something this big. He helped manage his money, and he was determined to help manage his love life. Cole had been given ample opportunity to find love on his own, but in Chad's eyes, Cole had failed.

"Are we still going out on the boat tomorrow, Cole? Cole has a big yacht down in San Diego. We are going for a cruise. Carly is going too."

Sarah knew what Chad was up to but decided to nibble on the bait too. "What kind of yacht do you have?"

Cole was embarrassed for Chad. "It's not a yacht. It's a Cabin Cruiser. Sleeps 6 in a crunch. I use it for fishing and sometimes to just get away. I like to take my sister and her family out to fish. My nephews love it, and my brother-in-law, Billy, is funny to watch. He is a terrible fisherman. Plenty of room for one more if you think you can make it. Besides, we wouldn't want to disappoint Chad and Carly, you know."

"No, best not to disappoint them. What time do you plan on sailing out?"

Chad and Carly could not hide their grins. Cole looked in their general direction for approval. "Is 9 AM too early?"

72

Carly stayed with her sister in hopes of prepping her for her date with Cole. She and Chad had thought of excusing themselves just before sailing, but after considering the risk, they thought better of it. It was a seventy-minute drive from Sarah's condo to Cole's slip at the marina in Del Mar. Carly expected the distance to be a barrier to the proposed relationship. Fears were somewhat alleviated when Sarah talked about some of her favorite places as they drove down the coast.

The sisters arrived in a spirited mood. Adorned in sundresses, wide floppy hats, and designer sunglasses, the girls exited the car to Chad's catcalls. Cole smiled and was glad he chose to dress in his civilian clothes. Sarah's eyes were glued to him. He was dressed like a cover model on GQ complete with Ray-Ban Wayfarer sunglasses and a wide-brimmed bucket hat to keep his face from being burned. He wore a long sleeve white linen shirt and a pair of light blue chinos from *Tommy Bahama*. Sarah thought he could have done better with the shoes, but she could overlook that.

The crew first found the boat to be smaller than expected. It was a large boat but it was dwarfed by much larger boats in the marina. Once out to sea, the girls were able to fully appreciate the room they had both above and below deck. Cole and Chad had decided this would not be a fishing trip since the girls were tagging along. As they cruised northward past Oceanside, the mountains reached the sky, and near vacant land dotted the landscape. They made their way further north and in another hour they pulled into a marina in Newport Beach. The group made their way to a *Michelin-awarded* restaurant that Carly had discovered on the internet. Sarah knew that Carly had married into wealth, but this seemed to confirm it.

They spent an hour on a terrace overlooking the Pacific Ocean. Cole and Sarah had the *Classic French Omelet* while Chad and Carly shared three items that Cole and Sarah couldn't even pronounce. After brunch, the couples strolled through the shops of Lido Marina. Wine and cheese were purchased for the afternoon return trip, and the couples made their way back to San Diego.

The return trip was more leisurely. Cole knew that Chad was experienced at the helm so he let him play captain on the way back. Chad's pace was much slower. Cole and Sarah sat on the rear deck and enjoyed the wine. Cole pointed out a school of dolphins and a few blue whales. They were dressed appropriately for the season, but Sarah was a little cool. Cole noticed she was rubbing her arms through her knit sweater. He reached his arm around her and drew her near.

"Is that better?" The cup of sand in his voice was back.

"Yes. This is nice. You know you are nothing like I remember. I don't mean it in a bad way. You were always so quiet in school."

Cole briefly considered his next moves. "Well, I remember that you didn't want to have anything to do with me. After all, we were two grades behind. Doesn't seem like much now, does it?"

"No, it doesn't." Her head melted into his shoulder and his hug became more sensual.

The winds were shifting again for Cole. He had felt warmer in the years since he moved on from his time in Foster Creek. He was ready to take a chance now. He knew Sarah was not catch and release. She had a career and was way more together than the gals he picked up at the bars around the base. His only reluctance was giving Chad the satisfaction of an *'I told you so.'* He was still a practical man having never had these feelings before. He was reluctant to get too far ahead of his skis. This was a first date after all. *Oh My God, is this a date?*

B-dum.

B-dum.

B-dum.

The beat was steady and he felt it through his soul. It was different now; pleasant and calming. He didn't want to lose the rhythm.

"This is *very* nice." Cole glanced toward Chad and Carly and saw they were focused on the coastline. Sarah moved her head from his arm but still maintained no space between them. She finally moved her head toward him and Cole moved his hand to cup her cheek and leaned forward. And when Sarah returned his kiss, their journey began.

73

Cole sought harmony like the harmony that can only be present when the notes on a guitar are all in tune. Choices can always be made about the notes to be played or avoided. Several strings can be plucked with the same fierce stroke of a pick, but they can produce very different emotions. The thick strings at the top vibrate more aggressively, producing a rich bass sound. As one's life moves along like the plucked string that sits over the frets, the amplitude increases and the string has to work even harder to return to rest. Cole was both blessed and cursed to have lived a life on the low E string. Cole's string had been picked often, sometimes violently, but lately, his sounds were more like smooth jazz. He had adjusted to adulthood. He had a career and he was in love. He would not tell Sarah of the terror from his teenage years. That was a stage in his life that he hoped to forget. Smooth jazz. This is the genre he wanted to stay married to, but soon it would be time for Cole to dance to a music that was foreign to him.

After 25 years in service to his country, Mike Levy officially retired in 1992. Mike, Jr. was three at the time. CWO Levy was assigned to a local Navy recruiting office near Sante Fe two years prior. He had the option of teaching at a Navy School, but he opted for a less demanding post. It was a steady nine to five, and it was required since Vicki had deserted him. He quickly found the job boring, but there were no other options that would work for Junior. Mike Levy decided for his younger son's sake.

Mike knew his son would face an uphill battle if he knew the truth about his mother. He decided early on to grant Vicki's request. When

Junior finally asked about his mom, he would tell him that she passed away when he was an infant. Breast cancer seemed reasonable. Mike Senior would paint the picture of a loving, devoted wife and mother that would do anything for her son.

After retirement, Mike had more time for Junior. He consulted with Navy contractors and made far more money working part-time in the private sector than his full-time Navy salary. Still, he seemed unfulfilled and soon found his way back to womanizing. It was awkward at first. Junior was still young and required babysitters when Mike went out. Tucking Junior in became less frequent as the years went by.

It was in the summer of 2003 when Vicki Levy emerged from under her rock. Junior was fourteen and had already experimented with drugs and alcohol. When she introduced herself to him, he went all in on the drugs. His relationship with his father deteriorated, and he could never forgive him for what he saw as an unforgivable deception.

Mike was able to get a court-ordered restraining order against Vicki. He had the note Vicki had left him when she abandoned them, and after showing the judge, the judge granted the restraint. Vicki would not be allowed contact until Junior was eighteen.

Juvenile court became a regular venue for Junior. After three appearances in one year, the judge finally ordered a thirty-day stay in juvenile detention. Senior was at his wit's end. After Junior's release, Mike decided to tell Junior the whole truth, at least as he perceived it, about his life before Vicki.

Soon after, Junior used the broadband connection at the library and searched for COLE LEVY NAVY. Three results came back. There was a wedding announcement for Sarah Stoltz and Cole Levy. In the picture, Cole had a similar facial structure as Junior, so Junior took the information from the announcement and investigated further. He saw that Sarah was from Charleston, South Carolina, and he knew that couldn't be a coincidence.

He typed COLE LEVY SAN DIEGO in the search box.

This time, Junior was able to learn that Cole Levy was a graduate of the University of California, San Diego. He learned that the wedding was planned for June of 2004. That was now only a month away. He then clicked on a link to public records where he discovered the registration of a boat in San Diego County, California. Further research yielded several pictures from a brochure from *Wellcraft*. Junior surmised that Cole appeared to have successfully navigated his life without their father's help.

Junior then searched for EMILY LEVY. None of the results seemed to match. He then typed BILLY MCCASTER EMILY. After reading through the results, he concluded that the Billy and Emily McCasters of San Diego were his. A quick search through *Myspace*, and he had an email for Emily.

To: Billysgirl88@AOL.com
From: Juniorlevy89@gmail.com

"You don't know me. I didn't know about you until a few days ago. If you are the Emily Levy with a brother named Cole and a piece of shit father named Mike, please email me back. Our dad is ruining my life."

The End